A MATE FOR YORK

The Program Book 1

CHARLENE HARTNADY

Published by Charlene Hartnady
PO BOX 456, Melrose Arch,
Johannesburg, South Africa, 2176
charlene.hartnady@gmail.com

1

CASSIDY'S HANDS WERE CLAMMY and shaking. She had just retyped the same thing three times. At this rate, she would have to work even later than normal to get her work done. She sighed heavily.

Pull yourself together.

With shaking hands, she grabbed her purse from the floor next to her, reached inside and pulled out the folded up newspaper article.

Have you ever wanted to date a vampire?

Human women required. Must be enthusiastic about interactions with vampires. Must be willing to undergo a stringent medical exam. Must be prepared to sign a contractual agreement which would include a non-disclosure clause. This will be a temporary position. Limited spaces available within the program. Successful candidates can earn up to $45,000 per day, over a three-day period.

All she needed was three days leave.

Cassidy wasn't sure whether her hands were shaking because she had to ask for the leave and her boss was a total douche bag or because the thought of vampires drinking her blood wasn't exactly a welcome one.

More than likely a combination of both.

This was a major opportunity for her though. She had already been accepted into the trial phase of the program that the vampires were running. What was three days in her life? So there was a little risk involved. Okay, a lot of risk, but it would all be worth it in the end. She was drowning in debt. Stuck in a dead-end job. Stuck in this godforsaken town. This was her chance, her golden opportunity, and she planned on seizing it with both hands.

To remind herself what she was working towards, or at least running away from, she let her eyes roam around her cluttered desk. There were several piles of documents needing to be filed. A stack of orders lay next to her cranky old laptop. Hopefully it wouldn't freeze on her this time while she was uploading them into the system. It had been months since Sarah had left. There used to be two of them performing her job, and since her colleague was never replaced it was just her. She increasingly found that she had to get to work way earlier and stay later and later just to get the job done.

To add insult to injury, there were many days that her a-hole boss still had the audacity to come down on her for not meeting a deadline. He refused to listen to reason and would not accept being understaffed as an excuse. She'd never been one to shy away from hard work but the expectations were ridiculous. Her only saving grace was that she didn't have much of a life.

There had to be something more out there for her – and a hundred and thirty-five thousand big ones would not only pay off her debts but would also give her enough cash to go out and find one. A life, that is, and a damned good life it would be.

Cassidy took a deep breath and squared her shoulders. If she asked really nicely, hopefully Mark would give her a couple of days off. She couldn't remember the last time she had taken leave. Then it dawned on her, she'd taken three days after Sean had died a year ago. Her boss couldn't say no though. If he did, she wasn't beyond begging.

Rising to her feet, she made for the closed door at the other end of her office. After knocking twice, she entered.

The lazy ass was spread out on the corner sofa with his hands crossed behind his head. He didn't look in the least bit embarrassed about her finding him like that either.

"Cassidy." He put on a big cheesy smile as he rose to a sitting position. The buttons on his jacket pulled tight around his paunchy midsection. He didn't move much and ate big greasy lunches so it wasn't surprising. "Come on in. Take a seat," he gestured to a spot next to him on the sofa.

That would be the day. Her boss could get a bit touchy feely. Thankfully it had never gone beyond a pat on the butt, a hand on her shoulder or just a general invasion of her personal space. It put her on edge though because it was becoming worse of late. The sexual innuendos were also getting highly irritating. She pretended that they went over her head, but he was becoming more and more forward as time went by.

By the way his eyes moved down her body, she could tell that he was most definitely mentally undressing her. *Oh god.* That meant that he was in one of his grabby moods. *Damn.* She preferred it when he was acting like a total jerk. Easier to deal with.

"No, that's fine. Thank you." She worked hard to plaster a smile on her face. "I don't want to take up much of your time and I have to get back to work myself."

His eyes narrowed for a second before dropping to her breasts. "You could do with a little break every now and then... so could I for that matter." Even though she knew he couldn't see anything because of her baggy jacket, his eyes stayed glued to her boobs anyway. Why did she get the distinct impression that he was no longer talking about work? *Argh!*

"How long has your husband been gone now?" he asked, his gaze still locked on her chest. It made her want to fold her arms but she resisted the temptation. *None of your damned business.*

"It's been a year now since Sean passed." She tried hard to look sad and mournful. The truth was, if the bastard wasn't already dead she would've killed him herself. Turned out that there were things about Sean that she hadn't known. In fact, it was safe to say that she'd been living with and married to a total stranger. Funny how those things tended to come out when a person died.

Her boss did not need to know this information though. So far, playing the mourning wife was the only thing that kept him from pursuing her further.

"What can I do for you?" His eyes slid down to the juncture at her thighs and she had to fight the urge to squeeze them tightly together. Even though temperatures outside were damn near scorching, she still wore stockings, skirt to mid-calf, a button-up blouse and a jacket. Nothing was revealing and yet he still looked at her like she was standing there naked. It made her skin crawl. "I would be happy to oblige you. Just say the word, baby."

She hated it when he called her that. He started doing it a couple of weeks ago. Cassidy had asked him on several occasions to stop but she may as well have been speaking to a plank of wood.

She grit her teeth for a second, holding back a retort. "Great. Glad to hear it." Her voice sounded way more confident than she felt. "I need a couple of days off. It's been a really long time—"

"Forget it," he interrupted while standing up. "I need you... here." Another innuendo. Although she waited, he didn't give any further explanations.

"Look, I know there is a lot to do around here especially since Sarah left." His eyes clouded over immediately at the mention of her ex-colleague's name. "I would be happy to put in extra time."

As in, she wouldn't sleep and would have to work weekends to get the job done.

"I'll do whatever it takes. I just really need a couple of days. It's important."

His eyes lit up and she realized what she had just

said and how it would've sounded to a complete pig like Mark.

"Anything?" he rolled the word off of his tongue.

"Well…" It came out sounding breathless but only because she was nervous. "Not anything. What I meant to say was—"

"No, no. I like that you would do anything, in fact, there is something I've been meaning to discuss with you." His gaze dropped to her breasts again.

Please no. Anything but that.

Cassidy swallowed hard, actually feeling sick to her stomach. She shook her head.

"You can have a few days, baby. In fact, I'll hire you an assistant." Ironically he played with the wedding band on his ring finger. His voice had turned sickly sweet. "I'd be willing to go a long way for you if you only met me halfway. It's time you got over the loss of your husband and I plan on helping you to do that."

"Um… I don't think…" Her voice was soft and shaky. Her hands shook too, so she folded her arms.

This was not happening.

"Look, Cass… baby, you're an okay-looking woman. Not normally the type I'd go for. I prefer them a bit younger, bigger tits, tighter ass…" He looked her up and down as if he were sizing her up and finding her lacking. "I'd be willing to give you a go… help you out. Now… baby…" he paused.

Cassidy felt like the air had seized in her lungs, like her heart had stopped beating. Her mouth gaped open but she couldn't close it. She tried to speak but could only manage a croak.

She watched in horror as her boss pulled down his

zipper and pulled out a wrinkled, flaccid cock. "Suck on this. Or you could bend over and I'll fuck you – the choice is yours. I would recommend the fuck because quite frankly I think you could use it." He was deadly serious. Even gave a small nod like he was doing her a favor or something.

To the delight of her oxygen starved lungs, she managed to suck in a deep breath but still couldn't get any words out. Not a single, solitary syllable.

"I know you've had to play the part of the devastated wife and all that but I'm sure you really want a bit of this." He waved his cock at her, although wave was not the right description. The problem was that a limp dick couldn't really wave. It flopped about pathetically in his hand.

Cassidy looked from his tiny dick up to his ruddy, pasty face and back down again before bursting out laughing. It was the kind of laugh that had her bending at the knees, hunching over. Sucking in another lungful of air, she gave it all she had. Unable to stop even if she wanted to. Until tears rolled down her cheeks. Until she was gasping for breath.

"Hey now…" Mark started to look distinctly uncomfortable. "That's not really the sort of response I expected from you." He didn't look so sure anymore, even started to put his dick away before his eyes hardened.

Cassidy wiped the tears from her face. She still couldn't believe what the hell she was seeing and even worse, what she was hearing. *What a complete asshole.*

Her boss took a step towards her. "The time for games is over. Get down on your knees if you want to keep your job. I'm your boss and your behavior is just plain rude."

Any hint of humor evaporated in an instant. "I'll tell you what's rude... you taking out your thing is rude. You're right, you're my boss which means what is happening right here," she gestured between the two of them, looking pointedly at his member, "is called sexual harassment."

He narrowed his eyes at her. "Damn fucking straight, little missy. I want you to sexually harass this right now." He clutched his penis, flopping it around some more.

"Alrighty then. Let me just go and fetch my purse," she grinned at him, putting every little bit of sarcasm she had into the smile.

"Why would you need your purse?" he frowned.

"To get my magnifying glass. You have just about the smallest dick that I've ever seen." Not that she had seen many, but she didn't think she needed to. His penis was a joke.

It was his turn to gape. To turn a shade of bright red. "You didn't just say that. I'm going to pretend that I didn't hear that. This is your last fucking chance." Spittle flew from his mouth. "Show me your tits and get onto your fucking knees. Make me fucking come and do it now or you are out of a job."

"You can pretend all you want. As far as I'm concerned you can pretend that I'm sucking on your limp dick as well, because it will never happen. You can take your job and your tiny penis and shove um where the sun don't shine!" Cassidy almost wanted to slap a hand over her mouth, she couldn't believe that she had just said all of that. One thing was for sure, she was done taking shit from men. *Done!*

She gave him a disgusted look, turned on her heel and walked out. After grabbing her purse, she left without looking back, praying that her old faithful car would start. It hadn't been serviced since before her husband had died and it wasn't sounding right lately. The gearbox grated sometimes when she changed gears. There was a rattling noise. She just didn't have the funds. That was all about to change though. She hadn't exactly planned on leaving her job just yet. What if things didn't work out? She'd planned on keeping her job as a safety net instead of counting chickens she didn't have. It was too late to go back now.

Despite her lack of a backup plan, Cassidy grinned as her car started with a rattle and a splutter. Grinned even wider as she pulled away, hearing the gravel crunch beneath her tires. Now all she had to do was get through the next few days and she was home free.

2

YORK WATCHED FROM THE sidelines as Lazarus punched the other male repeatedly in the face until he fell to the ground unconscious. His friend raised his bloody fists into the air and roared triumphantly.

"Aren't you glad that you don't need to get involved in all of this?" Brant sounded bored as he waved a hand in the direction of the fighting males. Most of the elite guard were assembled together to fight for an opportunity to be included in the breeding program.

The whole place reeked of testosterone, adrenaline and blood. Didn't get much better.

York could not understand how some of the males had decided not to be included. Who would not want a mate and a chance at offspring? It was highly unfortunate that most of the vampire females were unable to birth young. It was therefore necessary that such a program existed.

A human female.

His pulse increased and everything in him tightened. What a prize. He'd always dreamed of an opportunity such as this. Could not wait until it became a reality.

Something was bothering him though. York turned to face Brant. "There is something I have been meaning to discuss with you, my lord."

His king turned dark eyes towards him. "Yes? Have you changed your mind about a place in the dating program?"

He shook his head. "Never," he growled. "I thought it was called the breeding program." He felt himself frown.

"I'm glad to hear it. My public relations team has recommended that we change the name to dating program… " He pulled a face. "Humans are such timid creatures. We are all driven to mate and procreate. 'Breeding program' is a truthful and apt description." He sighed loudly. "Due to the bad press and fear the word 'breeding' evokes in humans, we have relabeled it Dating Program or The Program for short." His eyes darkened. "If you still want to be a part of the program, then what is it that you want to talk to me about?" Brant looked mildly interested.

The sound of meaty thuds and grunts drew his attention back to the fighting males. It seemed that one of the younger of the elite, Griffin, was a real contender and might just garner himself a place in the program. He had always enjoyed the lighthearted nature of the younger male and hoped that he did in fact make the top ten. It was certainly entertaining watching how he exchanged blows and gracefully avoided being hit.

"I am truly grateful to have been given a place in the trial phase of the program." York needed to tread carefully. Brant was known to have a short temper. York had granted Brant's younger brother, Xavier, a favor some time back. The agreement was that York would be given a position in the breeding program in return. The only thing he needed to do was to pass the trials.

Bloodlust.

It was a known fact that a percentage of the vampire population suffered from the affliction. The exact percentage, however, was unknown as vampire/human relations had always been banned. The affliction turned calm, collected vampires into blood-crazed maniacs liable to drain a human of their blood within minutes.

Brant nodded, his jaw clenched. The king was impatient as always.

"I think that it would be better if I fought for my place as well. I do not want to be looked down on by my peers. The last thing I want is for them to think that I've had an unfair advantage over them. That I'm not worthy to take a human mate."

His king's expression remained unreadable. "You do have an advantage and should take it and not worry so much about what others think. You do realize that you could lose your place should you decide to fight?"

York had to hold back a laugh. "Highly doubtful, my lord. I am one of the top elite warriors. There are ten spots available in the program." He shrugged. "It's a no-brainer. I'm not worried."

Brant looked him up and down. "You're a cocky bastard," he growled before grinning. "I like that." Then he looked thoughtful for a moment. "Xavier mentioned that you have wanted a human female and a family of your own. That this has been a dream of yours for a very long time." His whole expression softened, which was strange to York. His king was never emotional or sentimental. "It's wonderful... having a son is better than I ever thought it would be. Are you sure that you are willing to risk that? Human females are..." If his expression was soft before, it was positively gooey now and York was tempted to ask his king to stop. He looked just plain freaky with that expression on his face. "My little human is the best. They are full of nonsense, but it only adds to their appeal. Their scent is out of this world. Right now, you are guaranteed a place. I don't think I would risk it."

"Like I said before, there is no risk." Even now, York felt the adrenaline surge through his body at the thought of a fight. He felt his muscles bunch beneath his skin in preparation. Grinding his teeth, he slammed his fist into his open hand.

"Be my guest, but know that should you lose, you forfeit your place." Brant's eyes darkened.

"I understand, my lord." York dipped his head as a show of respect and thanks. He then made his way to where the action was.

The crowds were thick. A male fell to the left of him, his lip split open and his eyes swollen shut, yet he still clawed his way to his feet only to be slammed back down again. York kept on walking, his gaze fixed on the largest of the elite males.

"I thought you had decided that being a pussy was more your style," Lazarus said, his eyes glinting with humor.

"I eat pussy," York growled, looking down at his chest and arms. "Nope... no pussy here."

Lazarus grinned. "I was starting to get disappointed there for a second. My biggest competition, sidelined by choice."

He and Lazarus were neck-and-neck for top position in the elite team. They were both big motherfuckers with Lazarus having a few more pounds on him. Where Lazarus beat him in bulk though, he won out in speed and agility. It just depended on which direction the wind blew as to which one of them would win a sparring bout on any given day.

Sparring was one thing; York looked forward to an actual no-holds-barred fight with his nemesis. He removed his shirt, making his intentions clear.

Lazarus leaned back against the wall behind him. "You would have one up on me though since this would be my second round in less than five minutes."

York choked out a laugh. "Are you talking about when you punched that poor schmuck a handful of times in the face before he fell down? It must've tired you out something fierce."

Lazarus' lip twitched. "I'm exhausted."

"Hang ten while I take one of the others down. Take a little breather, old man," York winked at Lazarus, whose smile died, "because I'm coming for you."

"I'm ready for you now," Lazarus growled.

"I insist, wouldn't want to say I had the unfair

advantage. I have to say that you really are looking a little tired. Should I call a healer?" Fuck, he loved this shit. Loved the way the other male's face clouded in anger as he charged at York. It was another small advantage he had over the male – Lazarus had a temper that got away from him sometimes. Made him do stupid things.

A sudden blind charge was one of those dumb things. York sprang out of the way at the last moment and kneed Lazarus in the head, using the other male's momentum against him. The male dropped like a stone, hitting the ground with a loud crash.

York didn't wait for him to recover, he kicked him hard in the midsection twice, hearing a rib crack. Now that he had the upper hand, he took a step back, allowing his opponent to get to his feet. Every single breath would be like a stab to the chest and his head had to hurt like a bitch.

He noticed that Lazarus was in fact taking shallow breaths, that his face had paled significantly. It took a little longer for bone to regenerate. Even so, York knew he didn't have much time.

"You're a dick!" Lazarus spat a mouthful of blood on the ground at his feet.

"I told you to watch that temper of yours." York threw him a wide grin, which he knew would piss the male off.

Lazarus' dark eyes turned stormy as he attacked again, throwing a wide right hook that missed by a mile. With precision and focus, York landed two tight punches to his solar plexus. The air left Lazarus' lungs in a *whoosh* and his eyes widened.

It didn't stop him from head-butting York in the face though. Pain exploded in his nose and his throat filled with blood. Served him right for momentarily underestimating his opponent. It was time to end this.

York took two steps back as he steadied himself before launching himself at Lazarus with a double kick, first to the chest and then to the head. There was another snap, probably the same bone re-breaking. It had the desired effect. Lazarus grabbed ahold of his chest, groaning as he fell back. His nose was a flattened mess.

"Stay down," York growled.

"Fuck you!" Lazarus shouted as he staggered back upright.

York kicked the male again, this time going easy on him. "Lie down. You'll get into the program easily. I've won this round. You need to concede."

He shook his head in disbelief as Lazarus once again got back up onto unstable legs. "Don't say I didn't warn you," York growled under his breath. Using every last bit of strength he had in him, he kicked the male so hard that there was a loud crack as his neck snapped.

This time when he fell, there was no trying to get up. Lazarus would wake up in the morning with a bitch of a headache.

York motioned for one of the healers to come and assist.

"Ruthless. I like that," a familiar voice said from behind him. When he turned, Brant was smiling. "Think you're right, you'll definitely make the program on your own steam."

"Should've stayed down." York shook his head. Breaking his neck had been the quickest way to put him down without doing too much damage in the process. He could've pummeled his face and broken a multitude of bones in his body, thereby choosing the path of quickest healing with the least pain. Lazarus was a fine warrior and would understand though. He would be fighting fit in the morning and there was no doubt in his mind that the male would pick up one of the spots.

"You did what you had to do." Brant could be a cruel bastard. That was for sure. "Now, all you have to do is get through the trials. Human females taste so sweet. They're impossible to resist. We're predicting that at least two of the ten males who qualify will have bloodlust."

There was no fucking way that he had gotten this far only to not make the breeding program because of bloodlust. Thing was, it really did exist. Vampires who were affected with the affliction were a major danger to humans. Could not be trusted anywhere near them.

The trial period was designed in such a way that the top ten would drink from specially selected human females. Those who were unable to stop would be forcibly taken from the females and expelled from the program.

His throat tightened and his muscles bunched. Then he shook off the emotion. He was tough and had strong willpower. There was no way in hell that he had bloodlust. He refused to believe it. In just a few short days he would prove it.

3

HER BACK ACHED AS if it was breaking. Her arm felt like it was being stretched and pulled out of its socket.

Although she had one of those pulley bags, the wheels had long since seized so she had to carry it instead of being able to drag it. This type of bag was not exactly designed for carrying.

"I can't believe it's an honest to god castle," the woman next to her gushed.

"Crazy, I can't believe we're here." Another bounced up and down. She at least had a tidy rucksack on her back, which made such a movement feasible.

"This way ladies." A tall, really beautiful woman motioned for them to continue following. She'd introduced herself as Allison. Her skin was like porcelain and her lips were so red and lush that Cassidy struggled to take her eyes off them. She wasn't into women, but this woman almost had her re-thinking that decision. They walked for several minutes until they reached what looked like a back entrance to the castle. "Before we go any further, I just need to verbally confirm with each of you that you attended the training and signed off on your records."

Everyone nodded, acknowledging that they had.

Allison's mouth curved into a perfect smile. "Great stuff." She made a note in a book that she was carrying. "Lastly, I need to confirm that you've all initialed every page and signed the contract."

Again, all four of them nodded their heads.

"Are we really in that much danger?" one of the women asked. Cassidy couldn't remember her or any of the other ladies' names. She'd been far too nervous when they had been introduced to one another not ten minutes before. Crossing and uncrossing her arms, she realized that she still was.

"One of the clauses exempted the vampires from prosecution should one of us be injured." She chewed her gum as she spoke. "Should we be afraid? Are there precautions we can take?"

Allison raised her eyebrows. "Did you pay attention at the training session?"

"Yes, I did. It just became a lot more real now that I'm actually here though." She looked around them for a second or two before her eyes settled back on Allison. "Bloodlust, this whole drinking thing... quite frankly, I'm a little nervous now." Her eyes were wide and her brows were raised, she even stopped chewing for a second.

Taking a deep breath, Allison put a reassuring hand on the woman's arm. "You are right to be nervous. There is risk involved..."

Cassidy felt her heart-rate increase and her mouth go dry. Two of the girls gasped loudly, including the one asking all the questions.

Allison smiled warmly, looking at each one of them in turn. "We have taken every precaution. There are closed circuit televisions in every room and three guards posted just outside the door. If there is any doubt at all, even the smallest amount, they will be at your side in a second."

This seemed to sufficiently reassure another of the women, she looked to be the youngest and she broke out into a wide grin. "Is it true that we might orgasm," she giggled, running a hand through her shoulder-length hair, "while the guys drink from us? Does it really feel that good? Surely it can't be that good?"

Allison picked some lint off of her jacket, smoothing down the garment when she was done. "Yes, you will become highly aroused. All human females are greatly affected. If you are attracted to the male who is drinking from you, it heightens the experience." Again, the woman turned her big doe-like eyes to each of them. "It is nothing to be ashamed of. As you know, our males are not permitted to have sexual relations with you but they can ease you if you so wish."

Ease? What the hell did that mean? Unfortunately, she could guess.

"They can ease us?" It was the blond woman chewing gum who spoke; she didn't look too impressed. "As in put their hands on us?"

Allison nodded curtly. "It is entirely up to you. Whatever you do though, do not try and entice them into having sex. It will get them booted from the program, and both you and the male in a world of trouble. We have strict rules in place to protect you. Please remember this at all times. It was in the contract that you all have signed."

"I'm not interested in having sex with anyone." Blondie popped her gum. "I doubt I'll become aroused. I mean really," she huffed, tucking a loose strand of hair behind her ear.

The youngest woman sucked in a deep breath, her grin still firmly plastered on her face. "I think vampires are so hunky. My dad would kill me if I ever mated one…" She looked disappointed. "It's why I'm here for the trials and not for the actual breeding program. At least I will get to experience sort of being with one. What my dad doesn't know won't kill him." She looked to be in her early twenties. "I need enough money to leave home as well. I want my own place and waiting tables isn't going to get me there."

"I'm sure you will succeed." Allison looked pointedly at the young girl before lifting her eyes back to the group. "It is a known fact that human females find vampire males attractive. You will become aroused whether you like it or not. It's something that you will need to come to terms with before tomorrow." The vampire woman delivered the statement in such a matter-of-fact manner that Cassidy believed her. Of course, she had heard this during the training but dismissed it outright as exaggeration. Now she wasn't so sure. It scared the hell out of her. The last thing she wanted was to become aroused in front of a total stranger… *how embarrassing.* Her only consolation was that they had been informed that drinking would be over in less than half a minute. Not so long.

Blondie shook her head, popping her gum noisily. "They are not touching me and I am sure as hell not going to become aroused in any way whatsoever and that's final."

Allison nodded, clearly not buying a single word the other woman was saying. "Now, if you'll follow me, I'll show you to your rooms." They walked through the door, down the hallway and up a long flight of stairs. Then down another even longer hallway that led to another door. This opened to an outside foyer. There was a building up ahead. It looked like a French provincial style boutique hotel. Her arm was aching by the time they made it down the long path that led to the doors. She could see big, hulking figures posted just outside of it. More of said large figures stalked around the building perimeter. They were dressed all in black.

Cassidy's jaw dropped and she was at an utter loss for words for the second time in as many days. As they drew closer, she noticed that the men were the biggest, buffest, most badass specimens she had ever laid her eyes on.

Their heads turned towards them as they walked up. The closest guy winked at them. The younger woman giggled.

Allison seemed to sniff the air. *Weird.* "Now remember, ladies, no sex for the duration of your stay. We wouldn't want any of our males to lose a penis." All of the guys' heads snapped forward. The closest one swallowed thickly, his Adam's apple working overtime.

"You're joking right?" The woman who had remained quiet for the duration suddenly piped up.

Allison shook her head. "It would regenerate but it's a painful process, wouldn't you agree?" Her attention was on the closest man... um... vampire.

He looked pained for a moment, actually grabbing ahold of his package. Since he was wearing tight leather pants, she could see that it was a mighty large package at that. "Don't joke around at our expense, Allison. Play nice."

"No jokes and you all know it. Touch one of these females and you lose your junk. I hope I've made myself clear."

"Crystal," the closest guy growled. An actual growl. *Lord help them.*

There were grunts and mutterings from the other three, but they all nodded in agreement in the end. "We won't touch any of the females," the guy further down the way boomed. "Even if they beg!"

Arrogant much? She kept her thoughts to herself.

"As if," Blondie said between chews on her gum.

"Well, if you want to keep your balls neatly attached to your body, I suggest you listen. Regardless of the temptation." By the look in Allison's eyes, Cassidy could tell that she wasn't joking.

These vampires didn't mess around. She and Blondie were most definitely on the same page. She wasn't here to make any friends or to have any kind of sexual contact with a man –make that a vampire – either. It was her turn to swallow thickly. It didn't matter how phenomenally built and attractive they were. She was here to do a job and to earn a future for herself in the form of cold hard cash. Nothing was going to get in the way of that. Nothing. Sex was seriously overrated anyway and was the last thing on her mind. Scratch that, it wasn't on her mind at all.

There was a knock at her door.

Cassidy pulled a pillow over her head, she looked to the side and glanced at her watch. It was still at least an hour before dinner so that couldn't be it. The last thing she felt like doing was having to make small talk.

Her door was locked from the inside. With a sigh, she got up off the bed and went to open it.

"Hey." It was the young girl. "I'm really excited about all of this. Do you mind if I come in?" Her eyes were bright and shining. "I'm Deanne, my friends call me Dee."

"I'm Cassidy. Come on in." Maybe a little companionship wouldn't be so bad after all. The young woman seemed really sweet and her excitement was tangible.

"Do you mind?" Dee gestured to the bed.

"Not at all." Cassidy couldn't help but to smile back at her. The young lady had a grin about a mile wide.

Dee made herself comfortable on the bed, tucking her legs underneath her. "How awesome is this place?" She looked around the room with wide eyes.

Cassidy sat down on the edge of the bed. "Yeah, it sure is something." The room was more like a five-star suite. It was tastefully decorated with no expense spared, from the beautiful artwork on the walls to the plush woolen carpets. There was a silver bowl containing orchids on the corner table. Even the curtains looked like they were made from crushed silk and the finest lace. The furniture was made from real wood – the heavy expensive stuff, not the cheap plywood rubbish that she had at home. She forced herself to keep in mind that this lifestyle would only last a few days, she really didn't want to get too comfortable.

"My room is just as stunning. Do you also have a corner Jacuzzi bath as well?"

Cassidy nodded. "Yup."

"And you haven't used it yet?" Dee looked her up and down like she was smoking something.

Cassidy shook her head, noticing for the first time how the young woman's brown hair was a little damp. It had streaks of lighter chestnut when the sun caught the strands.

Pulling her legs more firmly underneath herself, Dee looked her in the eye. "So, I have to say, you look a little nervous. You were really quiet during training and again earlier today."

"We signed waivers giving the vampires permission to monitor our every move, the risks were made clear. You can't tell me you're not a little bit scared as well." Cassidy put her hands on the bed behind her and stretched back.

Dee shrugged. "I guess I am a little afraid, but it only makes it that much more exciting. Vampires are just so intense, so gorgeous. After seeing the guys outside, I have to say, I'm starting to feel a little upset that I didn't go for the actual program. I really wouldn't mind going the whole hog. I've heard that when vampires marry, it's for life." Her eyes twinkled before taking on a faraway look. "It's just so romantic."

Cassidy smiled, remembering what it was like before she'd met and married Sean. Before she'd found out what a lying, conniving asshole he really was. The young woman in front of her was pure innocence, she had yet to have her heart pulled out of her chest and stomped on. Cassidy found herself both envying and sympathizing with her.

Dee played with the frayed edge of her denim shorts. "Do you think it'll be as good as they say? I mean..." Her cheeks turned bright, bright red. "Surely it was an exaggeration." She didn't wait for Cassidy's response. "At least they have vampire women monitoring the camera feeds." She looked down at her thighs and continued to pull on one of the frayed pieces. "Would you let them touch you? I mean, if you really liked one of them?"

Cassidy swallowed hard. "I guess I've always been a bit old-fashioned. I kind of like to have dinner and a bit of dancing before I.... Actually, come to think of it... I like to date a guy for a good couple of weeks before I'll let them touch me like that. My only hope is that they were exaggerating when they talked about the attraction." There was a definite niggle inside of her. Chances were good that she was going to become aroused, she only hoped that it didn't get so bad that she'd lose control. Cassidy shook her head. "No, I definitely won't let anyone touch me."

The bed rocked as Dee repositioned herself, crossing her legs in front of her. Her toenails were bright pink. She chewed on her bottom lip for a few beats. "I had a boyfriend for two years, we recently broke up."

"Oh, I'm sorry to hear that." *What the hell was she supposed to say to that?* It seemed that Dee was one of those women who enjoyed telling her whole life story. Then again, maybe it was just this crazy situation that made her feel like confiding in someone and since they weren't allowed their cell phones for the duration of the stay, that didn't leave too many options.

"Don't be. I broke it off with him," Dee smiled. "He was a really nice guy, I liked him very much, but he couldn't make me... you know. I guess we weren't very compatible sexually." She scrunched up her face for a few moments, deep in thought. "Then again, he always seemed to enjoy himself immensely. All that grunting and groaning, the way his face would turn red and sweaty. It was gross. I would just lie there for the two or three minutes that it lasted. Then he kind of tensed up and moaned and that would be the end of that."

Cassidy found herself nodding in agreement. She knew the drill and Dee's description of sex was all too familiar. She'd only had one boyfriend before Sean and he was really useless. As it stood, Sean had only made her come a handful of times during their four years of marriage. Men could be so selfish.

The young lady chewed on her lip for a while before continuing. "I have experienced an orgasm." She paused for a long while. "All by myself," she giggled. "The thing is, I wouldn't mind having one... another way I guess. I mean, I wouldn't mind having one with someone else's help, you know?" A deep flush crept up from the neckline of her shirt.

"You are young," Cassidy said. "There are better guys out there, I'm sure." *Yeah right!* She didn't believe what she was saying herself, so how could she expect Dee to believe her. "What I'm trying to say is, at your age, there must be plenty of young men. You don't have to let a vampire touch you to get off."

"How old are you then?" Dee lifted her brows and clasped her hands over her lap.

"I'll be thirty next month." The 'big 30,' she couldn't believe it. A wave of sadness washed over her. By now she really had hoped to be settled down with the man of her dreams with at least two if not three children running around. The pain inside her only increased. So she gave herself a mental shake of the head and moved on. It was no use thinking along those lines. It just ended up hurting too damned much.

"That's still really young. I'm only five years younger than you, you know?" Dee smiled more widely. She really was sweet. Cassidy could not believe that so few years separated them. Had she really turned into such a cynical old woman in such a short time?

"I don't feel all that young," Cassidy said. "But I guess I still am." She smiled back at the young woman. This was a new beginning for her and she was going to embrace it. So what if she got a little horny? There was no way she was going to act on it.

In three days time, she would be in a position to start over. Then she'd do fun things again. Crazy things like swimming naked and watching the sunrise after staying up all night.

Dee let out a deep breath. "I'm going to do it." Her eyes were wide and sparkled with excitement. "I'm going to let one of them touch me. Live on the edge for once. I'm still young, still carefree." She threw her head back and laughed like a mad woman. Cassidy found herself laughing softly as well.

"I'm going to do it. I really am," she spoke more to herself than to Cassidy. "If I don't, I think that I'll always regret it. You know what I mean?"

Cassidy nodded. She knew exactly what Dee meant. Her being a part of this trial was much the same. If she hadn't done this, she would've regretted it. She was glad she was here. Glad even that she'd let Dee into her room, because she felt a little bit better now about the whole thing.

4

THERE WERE TWO CLOSED doors side by side. One was marked A and the other B. Cassidy looked down at the document in her hand, already knowing what was written there. Her first appointment was at ten o'clock in room A. She was a few minutes early. There were three guards outside each door. They looked much the same as the guards who were posted outside their building. Tall, built and cocky – literally. Every male vampire she had seen thus far was wearing leather pants and a leather shirt. The clothing fit like a second skin. Showing each and every sinewy muscle and bulge to perfection.

She'd seen a couple of the vampire women as well and wow... just wow! It actually made her feel sorry for the human women who had signed up to become mates to these men. There was simply no comparison. The only way to describe it was to take the most beautiful models, with their tall, slender figures and flawless skin and make them even more attractive and then you had a vampire woman. They oozed sex appeal from every pore.

There was the sound of hard footfalls behind her, Cassidy turned and watched as a forbidding specimen approached. His eyes were flinty and there were frown lines on his forehead. "Good morning. I'm Gideon and this is my team. We are here to ensure your safety today."

Cassidy swallowed hard and nodded, not sure that she could trust her own voice. *Crunch time.* She sucked in a deep breath and told herself over and over that she could do this. There was no other choice. It's not like she had a job to go back to.

"Do not be afraid. Even if there is the slightest suspicion of danger, the three males stationed at the door will enter and retrieve you. We have practiced this and are able to do it in less than three seconds. Should you feel afraid at any time, say the word 'pumpkin' and within three seconds, we will retrieve you. However, if we fear for your safety at any time, we will do so anyway. Do you understand?"

"Pumpkin." Even though her hands were shaking and her heart was racing, she still found herself smiling.

The big vampire's lip twitched. "We had to come up with something that you wouldn't say in general conversation or in the throes of..." He looked to somewhere behind her before returning his gaze to hers. "Make sure you remember it and use it without hesitation."

She nodded. "Pumpkin. I won't forget."

Some of the tension seemed to ease out of him. "I

know that you have been informed that all of the rooms are monitored by closed-circuit televisions. Two of our females will watch the camera feeds during your session. I need to verbally inform you now that this was discussed in your training and that you have consented to this in your contractual agreement." His dark eyes stayed locked with hers.

She nodded.

"I require your verbal response, please," Gideon said.

"I understand and yes — "

Door B flew open with a crash. It was the blond woman who liked to chew gum. Tears were streaming down her cheeks. She looked completely distraught. Like she'd just witnessed a murder or something. "Oh, my god," she sobbed. "I can't believe that just happened... Can't believe it," she wailed. She was wearing a summer dress.

That's when Cassidy noticed the two bleeding puncture wounds on her neck. The woman locked eyes with Gideon and sobbed even louder as she made her way towards them. "I need to leave." Tears were streaming down her face.

Gideon's nostrils flared and she actually heard him sucking in a lungful of air.

Cassidy opened her purse and reached inside, pulling out a wad of tissues. She handed one to the woman, who nodded her head in thanks.

After blowing her nose and pulling herself together somewhat, she continued. "I can't do this."

Gideon folded his hands across his chest. "Allowing a male to ease you is no reason for embarrassment."

"How dare you?" she sniffed loudly. "I don't want any of your filthy bloodsucker hands on me. I hate all of you but I couldn't help myself." She broke down crying again. "Oh god…"

Gideon bristled, Cassidy could actually see the muscles bunch beneath the leather shirt he was wearing. He tensed his jaw for a few beats. "You lied. You stated on your questionnaire that you were not opposed to vampires. Not opposed to vampires and humans mating."

"So freaking sue me. I needed the money." Her eyes were wild and blazing. No longer upset, Cassidy could see that the woman was pissed. "I don't want any of your filthy hands on me… ever again. It's not worth the money. I'm leaving right now."

"Sue you…?" Gideon snorted. "Actually," his eyes darkened, "we may do just that. A female such as you deserves to be sued." He motioned to the guard closest to them who grabbed the woman by the arm. "You are free to leave but you will hear from our lawyers." His jaw was set. His eyes blazing. "You lied… committed fraud." He shook his head looking disgusted.

"Escort this female from the property," Gideon growled. Low and deep. It sent shocks of fear racing through her body.

"Get your hands off of me!" Blondie shouted as they began to walk away.

Cassidy swallowed thickly. *What the hell?* Going through the door to room A didn't seem like such an easy task anymore. Not that she'd ever considered it easy in the first place.

Gideon smiled at her, flashing long ivory fangs that

almost had her shrinking away. "Apologies. You may go inside now." He gestured in the general direction of the building behind her. The one that housed room A and the vampire who would take blood from her.

This was it.

If she wasn't in such a bind, she'd turn around and walk away right now.

Cassidy was wearing another one of her work outfits, thick stockings, a blouse that was buttoned up right to her neck. Only this time she'd selected a thin knit sweater instead of the jacket. It was just too darned hot.

Cassidy glanced down at her watch. It was already five minutes past ten. This whole incident had made her late.

Swallowing hard, she walked over to the door and put her hand on the knob. Taking in a deep breath, she turned it and entered.

There was a man... vampire standing on the far side of the room. He turned to face her and she struggled to draw breath.

Holy hell!

It really wasn't fair. Why did the first vampire on her damned list have to be so good-looking?

From across the room, she could see that his eyes were the color of a clear winter's day. Crisp, bright blue. He was big, bigger than any of the guys she'd seen so far. His muscles had muscles. His hair was a dirty blond, cropped close to his scalp.

Her only consolation was that he seemed just as lost for words as she was. She watched his Adam's apple work. He clenched and unclenched his fists and licked his lips.

"I'm Cassidy." Her voice sounded shaky. Her whole body vibrated with both nervous tension and awareness.

"York." His voice was so deep, so rich, it almost had her falling to her knees and whimpering.

They had been told that only the strongest of the elite warriors were accepted into the program. They had been pitted against each other in one-on-one battles until only ten remained. There was no doubt in her mind that the vampire standing in front of her was one of the best. She didn't need to see an army of vampire warriors to know this to be true. He radiated raw energy and power. It was crazy, because some of the fear left her.

Surely the opposite should be true? Yet, it was almost like her fears from the last couple of weeks and certainly the last few days suddenly subsided.

"Where are my manners?" York said, walking towards her, his hand outstretched. His stunning blue eyes stayed locked with hers.

It was only out of sheer habit that she lifted her hand as he drew closer. His much bigger, much warmer one enclosed hers in a firm grip. She could feel that his fingers were rough and calloused, causing shivers to race up and down her spine.

York finally smiled and she realized that their hands were still clasped. Or rather, she was still holding on tightly to York's hand.

Without meaning to, Cassidy made a small squeaking noise and pulled her hand away. This was not just some good-looking guy; he was potentially a killer. There was no way in hell she was going to drool over him.

Not happening.

It didn't matter that his shoulders were impossibly broad. That his eyes held a mischievous twinkle. He wore faded jeans and a grey, nondescript T-shirt. Both garments clung to him lovingly.

No drooling.

She could do this.

"I can scent that you are a little afraid," he said, his deep voice washing over her like mulled wine.

"You can smell that?" *Stupid question, Cassidy.* It had been part of the brief during the training session that vampires had greatly enhanced senses. Their sense of smell was so fantastic that women wanting to join the program had to initially agree to go onto birth control pills to prevent ovulation. Apparently, the scent of a woman during that part of her cycle could drive a vampire male insane.

York nodded, his nostrils flared. "You had eggs and bacon for breakfast. Your shower gel is vanilla, your lotion is fruity and you're not wearing any perfume."

"We were told not to wear any. They said that it can be a little overpowering for your senses."

He nodded. "We have half an hour…" He glanced at the watch on his wrist. "Make that twenty minutes. Can I get you something to drink?"

Her mouth did feel a little dry but she doubted that a drink would help. She nodded anyway.

The room, just like her suite, was tastefully decorated. It was a living room with a small kitchenette in the corner. York moved to what looked like a minibar and opened it, having to duck down quite low to take a look inside at the contents.

"There is water, soda and juice…"

"A juice would be great, thanks." At least she was sounding a little more confident now, although the opposite was true. Allison said that if she was in the least bit attracted to the vampire drinking from her, her arousal would be that much worse. York had to be the most good-looking man she'd ever seen in her life. *He's not a man Cassidy, he's a vampire. He has long, sharp fangs that could rip you to shreds in an instant.*

Even knowing that, she couldn't help noticing how great his ass looked in his jeans. How thick his thighs were, how his built stature was that much more accentuated by his narrow waist.

"I've got orange, apple or fruit cocktail."

"Anything. Surprise me." *Why the hell had she said that?* He didn't even know her. *Stupid, stupid, stupid.*

York glanced over his shoulder at her. A small, mischievous grin toyed with the corners of his mouth. *Oh god!*

She thought of telling him that she hadn't meant to sound flirtatious, but bit her tongue instead. With her luck, it would come out sounding all wrong and just make things worse.

Ice chinked into a glass and there was a sound of a can opening. Grinning, York walked over and handed her the glass.

"You didn't mention tomato juice as an option." It looked just like blood. Her stomach gave a little lurch at the thought of this man's mouth on her neck… of his fangs piercing her skin. She also felt a heat low down in the pit of her stomach. Oh god, it was desire mixed with fear. The thought of his mouth on her both terrified and excited her.

"You said to surprise you, now drink up." York gestured to the glass in her hand.

Looking down at the beverage, she swallowed thickly, feeling a frisson of fear. If he went into bloodlust she was a goner. Three seconds suddenly felt like a long time. She wondered if she would even be able to say the word 'pumpkin.'

At the thought of the ridiculous safe word, she choked out a laugh.

York cocked his head. "What is it?"

She shook her head. "Nothing."

York scrutinized her for a second and she could almost physically feel his eyes on her. Stroking her flesh in the softest, most tantalizing way. She had to suppress a shiver.

"It's the safe word I was told to say if you end up... if you... you know." She shrugged, suddenly not feeling so amused anymore.

"Your safe word is funny. What is it?" Then he choked out a laugh of his own putting his hand up. "Don't say it or our session will be over before it begins."

"Don't worry, I won't," she smiled. "Unless of course..." She let the sentence die as she watched his eyes cloud for a second.

He looked away and when his gaze turned back to her, his eyes were more the color of the depths of the ocean. Dark, brooding, they radiated immense power. "You need to know that you are safe with me. I will not harm you in any way."

"How can you be so sure?" Her voice sounded a little croaky. It wasn't lost on her how her very life stood in the balance. There was a reason they were being paid so much money. Danger pay was the correct terminology.

He shrugged using just one shoulder, a half-smile played with the left side of his mouth. His bottom lip was full. It had the kind of lush softness a girl could suck on or bite into.

Bite.

Head in the game, Cassidy.

York gave a knowing smile. He had caught her checking him out. Her cheeks heated, which irritated her. It had been a very long time since a man had had this kind of effect on her. Who was she kidding? No man had ever had this kind of effect on her. Then again, York was not a man.

The vampire in question all-out grinned, making her knees feel a little weak. "I would never hurt you, Cassidy. Do I look weak to you?"

She found herself running her gaze down the length of him and shook her head. There was nothing but raw power. "You are far from weak, that's the problem. You could snap me like a twig."

He laughed. "No, a female like you," his eyes seemed to heat, "should be treasured and protected. It will be an honor to take your blood. I will not hurt you." His eyes dipped to her chest for the briefest second before moving back to her face. "You might want to lose the blouse." He pulled his own shirt over his head.

Her mouth dried in an instant and she found herself taking a sip of the juice. She had to force herself to relinquish her severe hold on the glass.

Thankfully, he didn't seem to notice how shaken she was or that she was staring. He turned to throw his shirt over the back of one of the sofas. York had a six-pack that looked like it had been carved from granite with that whole 'V' at the hips thing going on. His back was a wide expanse of hard muscle. He had those bulging muscles at the top of his shoulders. They ran down from his neck. The word *yummy* came to mind. Her tongue suddenly grew a mind of its own wanting to lick them... him... all over.

York turned to face her and flexed his pecs. Cassidy put a hand out, clutching for the edge of the sofa closest to her to steady herself.

His eyes dropped back down to her chest area. "You really should take that off – wouldn't want to ruin it."

"I... it's fine... it's old anyway." She was stuttering and stammering and still struggling to inhale sufficient oxygen into her lungs to be able to think clearly.

He frowned for a few seconds before nodding. "Maybe if we loosened the top two buttons." In less than two strides he was at her side.

It was probably her imagination, but she was sure she could feel heat radiating off of him. Heavens above, she could definitely smell his manly, musky scent with a hint of soapy, clean undertones. If cologne companies could bottle it, they'd make a small fortune.

"I'd be happy to help if —"

"No!" It came out a little too harsh. "I've got it. Are

you sure that I need to?" It would be better if she kept as clothed as possible and looked at him as little as possible. Her panties were distinctly damp and he had yet to lay a finger on her.

"I need to get to the base of your neck. Right about..." he lifted his hand, placing two fingers at her pulse just below the neckline of her blouse, "here." Her pulse sky-rocketed at the simple touch. She may not have been able to breathe earlier, but right now her breathing was too labored. Her chest rising and falling quickly.

"Hey..." His deep voice abraded her senses. "You're in good hands. Please calm down. I won't hurt you." Only then did he allow his hand to fall away from her. He looked down at her with such focus and intensity. Like she was the only person who existed in the world, or at least the only one who counted, which was crazy because they had only just met and this was a business arrangement.

"I know," she answered without thinking.

His eyes narrowed for a second. "Why are you so afraid then? I can scent your fear." His nostrils flared. "It's pungent."

"I'm sorry." Her cheeks heated and she looked away, feeling more vulnerable than she ever had before.

"You have nothing to be sorry about. If you truly believe that I mean you no harm, why are you still so afraid?" He paused.

How the hell did she tell him that she was attracted to him and afraid of becoming so aroused that she would do something that would embarrass the hell out of her? Images of straddling his lap, of his hands on her, rose up in her mind. Cassidy didn't do things like that with total strangers and wasn't about to start now. The problem was, she didn't think she was going to have much say in the matter, so maybe it was best that they discussed it now.

York cupped her chin, lifting her gaze to his. "Tell me." He released her.

Cassidy licked her lips. "I'm a little worried about my reaction to you when you drink from me."

His lips twitched.

"I'm worried because I've been told that we humans react quite strongly to being bitten." It came out rushed and high-pitched, but at least it was out in the open now.

York nodded once. "Yeah... you will become aroused and will need to be touched."

His candid, matter-of-fact approach had her taking a step back. She'd expected him to play it down or deny it flat out, but not this.

"Maybe take off the stockings and your underwear," he went on. "I am very good with my hands. I'll make sure that it is good for you."

Cassidy sat down on the sofa, landing heavily. He was being totally honest, which she appreciated. She shook her head. "No, it won't be necessary."

No way in hell!

Glancing down at her watch, she noticed that they had five minutes left before their session ended.

York gave her a cocky half-smile, hooking his fingers into his jean pockets. He was big, built and entirely hairless. Sexy wasn't nearly a good enough description. "It is a simple fact that when I sink my teeth into your honeyed skin, you are going to go out of your head with need. Your pussy will be wetter than it's ever been in your whole life. It will be like someone lit a match inside you. Your womb will scream to be filled. Your clit will throb. It will be torture to try and abstain – and there is no need to."

She shook her head, horrified at how turned on she was. How close she was to agreeing to everything. She hadn't had sex in a year. Right now that felt like a very long damned time.

York sat down next to her. "Climb onto my lap. Open your legs just a little. No one will see anything because you will be covered by your skirt." His voice dropped about a hundred octaves. "I will make you come multiple times in half a minute. It would be my pleasure."

He made it sound like he would be doing her a favor. Then again, he probably would be doing her a favor. Who was she kidding? Just look at the guy, there was no way he was interested in her in a real way.

She tried to eat healthy but the fact of the matter was, she enjoyed her food and wasn't about to give it up so that she could be a stick insect. As a result, she had some flesh on her bones; cellulite had also become a factor as she neared thirty.

Her brown hair was just past her shoulders. It was so dark that it looked black. It also had the tendency to be frizzy so she washed it daily using a special leave-in conditioner. It helped tame the frizz, mostly. Her boobs were a decent size but they were a little droopy. Thankfully her nipples still faced forward, so not too bad. She really couldn't complain. Her eyes were probably her best attribute. Somewhere between a light brown and green.

There was also nothing extraordinary about her. She'd had friends in school, but she was not one of the popular girls. She'd dated guys but never one of the really good-looking ones. None like York. Guys like York were always into the supermodel types, like the ones she'd seen around the castle. She was sure that the women they picked to enter the breeding program would be much the same. *He isn't interested in you, Cassidy, the delicious looking vampire is just being polite.*

"Can I help you undress?" York asked, bringing her back. "We don't have much time left."

"No, I'm good. Thanks." There was no way she would let him touch her out of some false sense of owing her. Or pity, or whatever it was that was driving him to have made the offer in the first place. *Forget it.*

York sighed loudly. "If you change your mind —"

"I won't," she snapped.

He held up his hands in mock surrender. "If you do by any small miracle decide that you need me to touch you, all you have to say is 'tiger' and I'll come to your rescue."

"Another word to remember," she had to laugh. "Thank you, but no."

"Just say the word and I'll ease you..." He winked at her. "I'm pretty sure that I can make you come even through all those layers of clothes. We have less than a minute so please get on my lap." He tapped his meaty thighs.

An argument was on the tip of her tongue but they

were out of time. She was about to lose herself fifteen big ones because of her fear of arousal.

Not happening.

Cassidy slid onto his lap and he steadied her by closing his hands on her hips. *Oh god, he was big and built and yummy.*

"The blouse," he growled. "The buttons," he added when she looked at him stupidly. His eyes were glowing and his voice was so deep. Even deeper than before. Her hands shook as she undid the top two buttons opening up her blouse to expose her neck.

"Relax and just say 'tiger' when it gets too much." His words were growled rather than spoken. Like his voice box was damaged or something. It was sexy as hell. When she looked down, she noticed that her silky blouse clung to her breasts. That her nipples were so hard that they poked right through her bra. *How embarrassing! Note to self, wear padded bra next time.*

York was the first vampire who was drinking from her today. There were two more to come. Just as she sucked in a deep breath, he bent down and sank his teeth into her.

There was a pinch, much like the feeling you get when a hypodermic needle breaks your skin. She made a squeaking noise followed by a low moan as he closed his mouth on her. His lips were hot and soft. His touch felt so sensual and intimate, it made her drag in a ragged breath.

His hands clasped her tighter, pulling her against his chest. Her own face was buried into the crook of his neck. His delicious, manly scent wrapped itself around her as his warmth seeped through her. When he sucked for the first time, her hands automatically closed on his arms, trying to find purchase. She tried to pull away but he held on tight. He groaned loudly, ending on a deep growl which vibrated against her, making her nipples harden to the point of pain.

When he sucked again, her back bowed and her girly bits turned wet. York had been right, dripping wet, wetter than ever before. She mewled like a kitten. Her grip on his arms increased but there was very little give because his muscles were so rock solid.

York growled loudly when he sucked again. The need to come became all-consuming. It felt like someone had lit a match inside her. She was burning with need.

Cassidy moaned. She could hear that her voice was dripping with sheer frustration. Panting, she pushed her thighs together to try and stop the ache. It only worsened the problem. On the next long pull, she cried out. This time her voice belied a need so consuming that it physically hurt.

Tiger.

One teeny, tiny word. No way was she letting him give her a pity orgasm.

Pumpkin.

If she shouted that word then the Calvary would come in and York would fail and be booted from the program. She couldn't do that to him. He'd been nothing but polite. Even his dirty talk had cut through the bullshit. It had been straight down the line honesty which was more than she had been afforded by any man in a very long time.

It only left one other option. She would wait this

out. This torture, this bliss, this nightmare. It would all be over soon. She only hoped that she could stay strong.

5

*B*LOOD.

Hot, thick, so sweet it had his muscles bunching and his dick turning rock hard. The female sitting on his lap had his blood boiling and his synapses firing on all cylinders. Her scent was beyond intoxicating. The taste of her blood was utter ecstasy.

In this moment, with her soft curves mashed up against him, with her gentle moans and whimpers in his ears, York was finally able to understand why bloodlust existed. He understood only too damned well what brought it on and why. He took a deep pull on her neck, his mouth filled with her rich blood. She moaned.

Any second now...

If he wasn't careful, he could lose hold of reality. If he didn't keep his wits about him he could lose himself in her taste, in the feel of her. Become swept away. What York had told this female was the truth. He would never harm her... *not ever.* Another deep suck and his cock actually twitched as she cried out. The sound a mixture of pleasure and pain.

Any second now…

His hands itched. His cock throbbed, wanting out of the tight confines of his jeans. It wanted to be buried deep inside this female. He longed to feel her wet heat. Her hands held him tight. Her little fingers dug into his biceps. She rubbed her thighs together, no doubt trying to ease the pressure that was building between them. It wouldn't help. Nothing would. He couldn't wait to touch her. Wished he could fuck her. The scent of her arousal had him groaning his own note of frustration. Another pull, this time he sucked deep, knowing that she would feel the pull in every erogenous zone in her body.

Any second now…

Her back bowed and she made a keening noise that almost made him throw her down on the sofa and rip her clothing to shreds. *How was she holding out?* When she'd first walked into this room, he had scented her fear, he had also scented her arousal. It had oozed from her pores from the moment she had laid eyes on him. The fear had come and gone as they initially talked, the arousal had only blossomed further. The female in his arms wanted him. She should not be able to fight this.

York wanted her just as much. The need to ease her was almost overwhelming. He wanted so much more than just a simple touch. Needed things that were not possible. He wanted to make her come. Hear her cries of pleasure. *Why was she being so stubborn?* Another long, hard suck had her holding her breath. He heard her heart stop for a few beats before starting back up again.

Give in...

Say it!

Another hard pull. He felt her little teeth sink into his flesh and he snarled. Need intermingled with frustration rode him hard. She bit hard enough for him to feel but not hard enough to break the skin. Desire and longing took ahold of him like never before.

It happened so quickly. One minute they were in an embrace and the next he was being pulled away from her.

Fuck!

York snarled in frustration as he caught a look of fear on her face. She was pale. One of the guards, he couldn't remember the fucker's name, had his arms around her slight shoulders.

"Mine," York snarled. His voice was so thick with rage that the word was mostly unrecognizable.

Cassidy shrieked in terror. She was afraid of him. The other two guards held onto him, one guard on each arm. Adrenaline coursed through his veins. His vision narrowed until only she remained. He had to get to the female. Had to show her that he meant her no harm, that she was safe.

He ripped his right arm free. Then, he elbowed the guard on that side. There was a sound of something cracking. More than likely the male's jaw. Then he punched the male on his left – the guard staggered back. Unfortunately, he could see from the corner of his eye that he wasn't injured enough to stay down. He loathed taking his eyes off the female but tore his gaze away long enough to punch him in the throat. There was a sickening crunch as the male's eyes bugged out of his skull. The guard would not die but he would back off, which was what York needed.

The stupid fucker that was touching the human pushed her behind him. "Don't do this, York."

"Fuck off," he growled.

"York, you are going to hurt the female."

There was no way he would ever hurt even the tiniest hair on her head and he was about to express this to the male that was in his way. He took a step towards them, preparing to remove the irritating fuck when a bolt shot through his body, it had muscles seizing. He fell to his knees.

"That should've knocked him out," a voice said. "I'm going to shoot him again."

"Wait." It was a voice he mildly recognized but couldn't place.

His eyes stayed locked on the human who stared at him from behind the guard. Her eyes were big, so beautiful. With a loud grunt, York began to rise back to his feet.

"Do it again."

His brow creased as he tried to place the voice but another bolt raced through him. His teeth clenched so tight that he tasted blood. His muscles tightened till they burned. His fingers curled until they resembled claws. It fucking hurt. He could feel the dark descend but fought it. He needed to speak to the female. Needed to tell her —

"This is the first damn day," a voice said. "The first day and I've already got shit of this magnitude." It was Brant. What was Brant doing in his room?

York struggled to wake up properly. His body felt heavy. His muscles ached.

"Nothing happened. We managed to contain it." The same voice he couldn't recognize earlier. His memories came crashing back. The human female, Cassidy, he needed to see her. Needed to explain. She was terrified of him.

He struggled to move, couldn't open his eyes to save his life. *Fuck!* He tried again… and again… until finally he felt his finger twitch. What the fuck had they done to him? His body felt used up.

"Fuck that!" Brant sounded pissed. "I have two guards down and a terrified human. I've had to pay her out for today even though only one male drank from her. She may not stay for the duration. We've already lost one female today, which would mean delaying the start of the breeding program while we bring in a replacement. Three females is the minimum."

That did it. York tore open his eyes and lurched upright. The thought of another male drinking from the little human had him feeling things he really shouldn't. It made him want to hit things. Made him want to hit other males… repeatedly.

What the hell was wrong with him?

It was lust. Not blood-fucking-lust. Just normal regular garden variety lust. The little human had fired his blood. He needed to explain what had happened earlier. He'd hated seeing the horror in her eyes. She truly believed that he was trying to hurt her, which was bullshit. Once she knew the truth, he could leave and get on with his life. Namely, he would meet with the females lined up for the breeding program. Once he was permitted to rut, he would fuck any thoughts of the dark-haired beauty right out of his mind. He would find a compatible female within the program and he'd have the family he'd always dreamed of.

Simple.

"Oh look," Brant smirked. "Someone decided to grace us with his presence."

"Where is she?" York had never been one for small talk, this was no time to start.

"The human you almost killed?" Brant raised his eyebrows. "Somewhere safe and far away from you."

"I don't have bloodlust." He worked hard to keep the growl from his voice. Brant was his king and commanded respect. "I didn't nearly kill her."

Brant all out laughed. "Like hell you don't have bloodlust. I watched the footage and you couldn't stop sucking on her neck. You actually got more and more agitated as time went on. All that snarling was a sure damned sign. You had to be dragged off of her and fought to get back. What was with the whole *mine* bullshit?" His face was hard and his eyes were as dark as night.

"I don't have bloodlust." This time he growled.

"What you have is a healthy dose of denial," Gideon chimed in.

"You fucking tasered me." York gave the male a hard stare. "It hurt like a bitch and was unnecessary." By the sting on his left butt cheek, he knew exactly where the darts had hit him.

"Our tasers hit at twice the human level. You were knocked with 100,000 volts of electrical energy and we had to shoot you twice to take you down." York glanced in the direction of the talking male. It was the guard who had touched Cassidy. York snarled at the fucker, exposing his fangs in warning. The male flinched and took a big step back.

Damn straight.

"Take it easy," Gideon said, looking concerned.

"I'm really sorry but I am scrapping you from the program," Brant said. "I know this meant a lot to you. It's just that we can't risk — "

"I don't have bloodlust. Did I enjoy drinking from her? Hell yeah! Did I like it when she bit me back? Abso-fucking-lutely. Did it send me over the edge? No way."

"Like Gideon said, you are in denial. I know bloodlust when I see it." Brant turned to leave. "This is not an argument. I've seen the footage." He glanced back. "You are out."

"I'll prove it!" York snarled, unable to help himself.

Brant stiffened and slowly turned. "It's too damned risky. Take a look at the footage for yourself," Brant shook his head. "You were out of control, York. I won't put another human back in the room with you. I won't do it." His king turned back and began to walk.

"I don't have to see the footage. I know it looked bad."

Brant kept on walking.

"Despite how it looked, I'm telling you that I know I don't have bloodlust. Give me another chance…

please." *Fuck!* How did he prove it? York swung his legs over the bed.

"Where do you think you're going?" Gideon asked, crossing his arms over his chest.

"I'm going to visit the human." He stood. Although he felt a bit stiff, he already felt better than when he had first woken up. Advanced healing was a wonderful thing.

"No, you're not," Gideon said, putting himself in the way of the door.

"Don't do this," York warned. "We both know you would lose."

"There are three guards outside your door, they all have a taser and will not hesitate to take you out. You will stay in this room until the trial phase is over. If you go anywhere near any of the humans once the program kicks off, I'm putting your ass in the dungeon."

"I don't have bloodlust. Why won't anyone listen to me?" Frustration caused him to pound his chest on the last word.

"It doesn't fucking matter. It's done. You're out." Gideon's eyes narrowed on him. "Why did you act the way you did?"

York couldn't answer the question. There was only one thing he knew for sure. "I enjoyed touching and drinking from the human... end of story. I don't have bloodlust."

"Not good enough. You don't have a logical explanation, do you?" Gideon let his arms fall to his sides.

"Not one that would make sense to you," York

finally said when he could see Gideon preparing to leave.

"Try me."

"I wanted her okay? The need to rut her rode me hard." He exhaled, sounding as frustrated as he felt.

"There's a reason it's called blood*lust*." Gideon shook his head. "Stay here, please." The male implored him with his eyes for a beat or two before leaving.

York snarled and punched a hole in the closest wall. This was a total fucking mess. The thing that aggravated him the most was that he kept on seeing a replay of Cassidy's wide, petrified eyes, he could still hear her shriek in terror. Anger and frustration coursed through him and he punched the wall a second time, leaving a wide fissure from floor to ceiling. A large chunk of plaster lay on the ground at his feet.

6

"**A**ND...?" DEE WHISPERED AS they sat down to eat. "How did it go? I didn't see you for the afternoon session."

Cassidy shrugged, not sure she wanted to even talk about the events of today. Her hands still shook and she actually felt cold despite the high temperatures. She shoved a forkful of food into her mouth instead. Steak, mashed potatoes and salad, normally a firm favorite. She didn't taste a thing though, just went through the chewing motions.

Dee licked some sauce off of her fingers and gave Cassidy a smile. "If you think I have the glowing look of a girl who got it all, you would be right," she giggled quietly, talking as softly as possible.

Cassidy shook her head but couldn't help but smile. "You have more guts than me, that's for sure."

Dee ate a mouthful of mashed potatoes before continuing. "I only planned on letting one of them touch me, but—" she shrugged, "I kind of let them all do it." She pulled a face. "It's not like I had sex with them or anything."

Cassidy took a deep breath. "Don't beat yourself up. It's hard resisting the urge."

"No, it's pretty much impossible. I orgasmed so many times, my eyes actually watered. And my throat hurts from the screaming." Come to think of it, Dee did have a bit of a huskiness to her voice that she didn't have earlier.

"Really?" Cassidy felt her eyes widen.

"Wait a minute, are you telling me that you were able to resist?" Dee pulled a lock of hair behind her ear.

"Um... yes..." She felt that she owed the other woman something in return. She really did seem very sweet. Cassidy cut a big piece of steak and shoved it into her mouth. Hopefully it would keep Dee from asking any other questions.

"I can't believe it. You resisted all three guys?" The other woman's eyes were wide and her mouth actually gaped. "You are much stronger than me. I am in awe of you. I also think you are a bit nuts because even though they barely touched me, the experience was off the charts good. I'm not even going to try and resist tomorrow."

Looking around the room, she noticed that the only other girl left in the program was nowhere to be seen. It was just the two of them. Cassidy took in a deep breath. It felt bad to allow Dee to assume that she'd had three guys drink from her. That she had managed to resist three times. "I only had one of them drink from me—" She shivered, remembering how good it had felt and not just the drinking part but also the feel of him. It was probably because she missed having someone in her life. She was lonely.

Dee frowned. "Why only one?"

Cassidy sighed. "He went into bloodlust."

"Oh, my god!" Dee shrieked, a small piece of steak shot from her mouth and she slapped a hand over her lips. Her eyes widened. "What happened? Are you hurt?"

Cassidy shook her head. "It was really scary. Not what I expected. He just started taking bigger and bigger sucks on my neck. Started making these grunting noises. Holding me tighter and tighter. Then the guards were pulling him off of me." She swallowed hard. "It's all a bit of a blur. He snarled and made these terrible noises. He fought the guards. His eyes were the scariest of all…" She took a deep breath, trying hard to calm herself. "They were glowing and wild. Like nothing I've ever seen before—"

"Glowing?" Dee sounded totally in awe.

Cassidy nodded. "He kept his eyes on me, even while he fought. It was like he wanted to tear me limb from limb. If they hadn't tasered him, I would be dead. For a few moments there I saw my life flash before my eyes." In that moment, she had realized what a pathetic existence she had lived. No job or real direction, no significant other. She had been the only child of older parents who both had passed away before her twenty-fifth birthday. Both her mom and dad were estranged from their families so no aunts and uncles or cousins. Her mother was a writer and her father a painter. Both introverts till the very end. Cassidy only had one real friend, but Julia had long since married and was so busy raising her family of three boys that they hardly got to spend much time together any more.

The emptiness had consumed her, especially since Sean had passed away. There was another reason, but it wasn't something she allowed herself to dwell on.

"That's terrible." Dee let her knife and fork fall down onto her plate with a clang. "I can't believe you're still here. I'm tempted to leave just hearing your story..." She chewed on her bottom lip for a few moments. "There I was having all these mind-blowing orgasms while you were almost killed. It could happen to any of us."

"Not that there are many left. Where is that other lady? The blonde who chewed the gum all the time left earlier."

Dee sucked in a deep breath. "Really? Why? Did her vampire also have bloodlust?" The other woman visibly shivered.

Cassidy shook her head. "It was nothing like that. She actually —" she paused.

"She what?"

"She let a vampire touch her and was pissed about it. She asked to leave and was escorted out."

Dee took a long drink of her soda. "Wow! She didn't like it? I can't believe that."

"I think she liked it a little too much if you ask me. She spouted some bull about vampires being disgusting bloodsuckers and told the head guard that she was just in it for the money."

"Yeah, there are a lot of hate groups out there." Dee shook her head sadly.

Cassidy nodded.

"It's so ridiculous, why can't everyone just get along?"

Cassidy shrugged. Her mother had been African American and her dad's family was originally from Scotland. She had to smile just thinking of him... of them. Her dad had orange hair and freckles and burned in the shade if he wasn't careful. They were so different from one another in so many ways, yet they fit together perfectly. They 'got' one another. Completed each other. Her dad had passed from a massive heart attack and her mom followed just one year later. She went in for corrective surgery for a mild hernia. It was a routine operation. She never woke up. The medical staff could not give a reason. Everything was textbook except of course for the part where her heart stopped. Cassidy was sure that it was from a broken heart. Not a day went by when her mom didn't mourn the passing of her husband. True love did exist, it was just as rare as a blue rose though.

"I still can't believe you are still here after going through such an ordeal." Dee's voice brought her back from her own thoughts.

"I need the money," she smiled at the younger woman. "Besides, the security team did a great job of rescuing me. York is one of the biggest vampires I've seen and they managed to keep me safe in the end."

"Good to know." Dee finished her soda, pushing the glass away.

Cassidy looked down at her still mostly full plate. She was suddenly really hungry. It had felt good to talk about her ordeal. It helped put things into perspective. York was out of the program, she'd been assured that she wouldn't see him again. The security team would protect her from any further incidences. Two more days and she'd be home free.

After a shower, she hit the sack. Flicking through the various channels until she finally settled on a mindless action movie, she managed to doze off, then woke up with a start. There was a woman screaming on the television. After glancing at her watch, she noticed that it was already a few minutes after twelve.

Cassidy switched on the side lamp and then pushed the button on the remote, watching as the TV screen turned dark. She used the toilet and made her way back to the bed. She had an early start tomorrow and would have her blood siphoned by no less than three vampires. Hopefully she wouldn't be as attracted to them as she was to —

A huge hand latched over her mouth and an arm snaked around her middle. She screamed against the palm, trying to pull herself free from the iron grip. There was no give. Her feet were hauled off the ground. Whoever was behind her was not only tall but solid. Like a brick shit house of gigantic proportions. Cassidy panicked, kicked out and even managed to nail her assailant a few times on the legs.

He grunted, pulling her more firmly against him so that she didn't have enough room to maneuver.

"Easy." His deep voice had her heart kicking into overdrive. It was him. The man – make that vampire – who had tried to kill her earlier today. It was York. She would recognize his deep baritone anywhere.

He was talking to her but she was too busy trying to get out of his ironclad grasp to listen. Sweat beaded on her brow. Her breathing was labored. She struggled to get sufficient oxygen through her nose. His hand was tight around her mouth. Cassidy had to save some of her strength. Trying to get away from him like this wasn't working. She sagged in his arms, acting like she had given up.

His big chest moved up and down behind her with each deep breath that he took. His mouth was at her ear. "I'm not going to hurt you," he whispered. "I came to explain about earlier. I came to apologize."

Yeah right. She'd seen the look in his eyes. It was as if he couldn't take his eyes off of her. She'd watched a documentary once about lions and how they stalked their prey. Even if there was a whole herd of deer, they would set their sights on one and then not take their eyes off of the target until it was trapped in its powerful jaws. Until it was game over.

That wasn't happening to her.

There were guards at the building entrance and more patrolling the grounds, she just had to alert them somehow.

"I'm going to take my hand away. I need you to trust me please, Cassidy."

Oh, sure! Like she'd trusted him before? *No way.*

"I won't hurt you." He whispered and for a second the emotion in his voice tempted her to believe him. It was stupid of her to have believed him the first time. Thing was, she didn't have much of a choice then. This time was different.

Cassidy tried to nod. Her action must have registered because he let out a great big sigh which tickled the side of her neck. Her nipples on her traitorous body hardened. Even after he'd tried to turn her into a snack basket earlier she still reacted to him on a base level. *Crazy-assed body.* It had always listened to her before. Why did it have to choose right now to grow a mind of its own?

"Okay, I'm letting you go now," his voice was still a husky whisper. His scent surrounded her. York smelled really good... for a psycho killer.

The moment his hand left her mouth she sucked in a lungful of air but he slapped the hand back in place before she could get much out. He cursed softly. "I told you that I won't hurt you." A deep rumble of sheer frustration. "I'm going to prove it to you."

Cassidy tried to shake her head. She tried to make a negative noise. There was nothing he could possibly do to change her mind about what had happened earlier. Her eyes widened and fear grabbed her in its icy tight grip.

She could hear her blood rushing through her veins. Could hear the sound of her own heart. Cassidy screamed into his hand as his mouth closed on her throat. There was a now all too familiar pinch and then a tightening of every part of her. She wasn't wearing panties, so wetness trickled down her thighs as he sucked on her again. Her clit throbbed. Her breasts ached. She was going to die in the throes of sexual frustration and it wasn't fair. She tried to scream, this time out of sheer desperation. She felt the emotion deep in both her body and her mind. Tears coursed down her cheeks. Of all the ways she imagined her death, this was not one of them.

York released her.

Released. Her.

It wasn't possible. From what she'd been told in training, if a vampire had bloodlust he couldn't stop himself. If left to his own devices he would suck a human dry in just a few minutes.

"I don't have bloodlust. Please let me explain," York said, his voice against the shell of her ear causing her to quiver in his arms. "Don't be afraid," he added, misconstruing her reaction as fear.

She nodded.

"We need to be quiet. If I am found here, I'll be in deep shit." This time, York lowered her to her feet before letting her go. Her legs shook, so he put out a hand and clasped her waist for a few beats. His touch didn't soothe her. It only made her feel even more edgy. God, she was wet down there. Everything still throbbed and craved. She slowly turned to face him and he relinquished his hold on her.

York was dressed all in black. Tight cargo-type pants, a long-sleeved top that showcased every hard-earned muscle to perfection, particularly his biceps and pecs. "I think you should go. You shouldn't be here," she whispered as softly as she could while putting as much meaning behind every word as she could muster. He needed to know that she meant business.

York nodded. "I know you don't want me here. I came to apologize."

They had to stand close so that they could whisper

and understand one another. Then again, it was probably mainly for her benefit since he had superhuman abilities. "Apologize... So you keep saying."

York took a deep breath before running a hand over the light cover of hair on his head. "I was an idiot." His eyes locked with hers. "I was trying to get you to say the word."

"You were trying to get me to say 'pumpkin'?" She could feel that her brow was furrowed, that her eyes were wide.

York grinned and actually gave a little snicker. "No wonder you were laughing earlier. It is a strange ass word to use as a safe word. Trust Gideon." He shook his head.

Cassidy found herself smiling despite the situation. Then York's eyes were back on her and she swallowed back her smile. Her breathing actually hitched. "No." Husky and deep. It did things to her that it really shouldn't. "Not that word, the other one."

"What other one?" She felt her frown deepen.

He looked at her pointedly.

"Oh, that one." Her voice came out sounding a little high-pitched. "Why would you want me to say that one?" She said it without thinking.

York swallowed thickly. His Adam's apple worked overtime and he shoved his hands into his pockets. "I really wanted to touch you. I know you wanted me, yet you wouldn't say the word."

It didn't make any sense. The big oaf was probably just used to getting what he wanted. His ego was bruised because she was one of the few women to ever actually say no to him. Maybe even the only one. "Look, York, just because you have women running after you twenty-four-seven doesn't mean you can have me."

York took his hands out of his pockets and folded his arms across his chest, his eyes dropped to her mouth and then to her breasts.

Oh crap! She was wearing her pajamas which comprised of sleeping shorts and a t-shirt with a little cartoon kitty across the front. It was tight and she wasn't wearing a bra. *Double crap!*

Cassidy folded her arms across her chest. His nostrils flared and she squeezed her legs closed. *Triple crap.* She also wasn't wearing panties and she was dripping wet.

They flared again as he inhaled deeply. "Explain to me why you are so damned turned on and have been since you first realized that it was me in your room. Even through your extreme fear, I could scent your arousal. You want me."

"I don't damn well want you and I don't need your pity orgasm, thank you."

"Orgasms." He gave added emphasis to ensure that she could hear that it was plural, which irritated her because her clit throbbed as he said the word.

"For the record." His eyes hardened up, his jaw was tense. Cassidy took a step back. "I would *not* have touched you out of pity. I would've touched you because I was rock hard for you just as I am right now. I would've touched you because you are one of the sexiest females I have ever seen. Your scent, your soft skin—" His voice was a deep growl. Low and dangerous. Simmering and seductive. She didn't think that he meant to sound that way but he did… in spades. "I was desperate to hear you say it, desperate to touch you." His eyes dropped to her mouth. "More than to just touch you." His chest heaved with each ragged breath. "The things I want to do to you…"

They both stood there for a few long seconds and she realized that he was waiting for her to speak. "Oh." Stupid thing to say after he'd broken into her room. After he had just said all those things.

York took a small step towards her and she had to force herself to stand her ground. "Well then?"

"Well then what?" she managed to squeak out.

"Which word is it going to be? Pumpkin," he gave a small smile, "and I leave, or tiger," he sucked in a deep breath, "and I stay." Her insides turned to mush.

"You can't be serious." She realized that she was panting softly. Her hands shook so she curled them up tight, folding her arms tighter against herself.

"I've never been more serious about anything in my entire life."

"What about your place in the program?" She was grasping at straws. Desperate to find a way to make him leave because she wasn't sure she could say no. Her body felt tight. So needy that she felt like she might burst at any second.

York shrugged. "I've been kicked out of the program." He licked his lips. "Pick a word little human. I can't wait to lick you… I only wish I could hear you scream my name when you come," he whispered.

She made a little whimpering noise and his eyes

started glowing softly.

York sniffed and narrowed his eyes. "Why are you afraid?"

"What's going on with your eyes?" He was looking at her in much the same way he had before when he had lost it.

"It happens when we are turned on. I want you really badly, Cassidy. You should see my dick. How fucking hard I am."

"Wow. Are all vampires so straight forward?" The crazy thing was that his dirty talk turned her on even more. She liked how direct he was. No bullshit.

York nodded. "Yeah. We are. Humans can be devious. They don't always say what they mean. You don't seem to have that trait. I need you to be honest with me now."

"It's just that we don't know each other. I don't have sex with strange men."

"I'm not a man, Cassidy." He cocked his head. "You seem to forget that. I'm a vampire male in his prime. I want you very badly and I can scent that you want me too. You need to know that I didn't come to your room with the purpose of fucking you."

She gasped at his use of the crude word because her desire increased at hearing him say it.

York smiled. "You're so timid. So sweet. I like that." He cupped her chin for a second before allowing his arm to fall at his side. "I came to apologize and to prove to you that I meant it when I said I wouldn't hurt you. I didn't want you to leave thinking that I hadn't been true to my word." He licked his lips. "Every time I come close to you or say the word 'fuck,' your scent becomes so — " He gave a low groan. "Makes me want to…" He lifted his hand, dropping it before he could touch her. "Just say something… what do you want? Must I leave?"

Yes. Go.

The words stuck in her throat because she didn't mean them. She shook her head.

"Thank god," he growled, stepping even closer to her. So close that they were almost touching. "Say the word. Let me touch you… please." His eyes were glowing again.

Her body was all systems go but she couldn't allow herself to be carried away by lust, to give in to such base urges. "It would be wrong," she sighed. Appalled to hear how disappointed she sounded.

"Do you agree that we have a strong physical connection?" His bright blue eyes bore into her.

Cassidy swallowed thickly and nodded. She'd never thought of it like that.

"It would be wrong to not explore this. I don't think I've ever wanted a female more."

Hearing him say those words broke down her last barrier, but she was still thinking clearly and there was something that needed saying first. "We can't have sex. My contractual agreement is clear. I can't afford to lose this job."

York cursed under his breath. "It's fine. At least let me touch you. Lick you. I want to feel your body tighten with your release… even if it is my tongue and not my cock that gets that pleasure." His gravelly voice made her so hot, she was sure she was going to self-combust at any second.

"Tiger," she whispered, shivering as she took in his answering groan.

York closed his mouth over hers, his tongue breached her lips. The kiss, just like the man, was hungry, raw and primal. She mewled into his mouth. There was a pull and a ripping noise. Her bare nipples abraded his shirt as he pulled her against him. He'd actually destroyed her t-shirt like an animal. Ripped it off her body. There was another tearing noise and her sleeping shorts fell around her ankles. From the sound of things, they were also destroyed.

She went from soaked to dripping wet.

York pulled away slightly. "We need to be very quiet," he whispered into her ear before pulling back further so that he could get a good look at her. His eyelashes fused as his gaze dropped down and swept over her body in a slow crawl.

Her cheeks warmed up a whole damn lot. At least the light was dim, as only the side lamp was on. She suddenly wished she hadn't eaten all of her heavy steak dinner as well as a bowl full of ice-cream for dessert. Every part of his body tensed and he growled loudly, snapping his mouth shut over the sound. York shook his head slowly, his eyes were so bright, it looked like he had been lit up from the inside. They turned hungry and fiery... so needy. "You're fucking perfect."

She could see that he meant every word. It gave her strength... made her feel really powerful. "Take off your shirt."

He nodded, his eyes stilled trained on her breasts.

"And the pants," she whispered.

York nodded again. Her boobs seemed to have him mesmerized. It made her grin but her smile died a fast death as he hauled down his cargo pants. His dick pulled forward as his pants slipped down and then snapped back against his abs. It was her turn to stare. To all out gape.

Thank god they weren't having sex because there was just no way that veined monstrosity would fit inside of her.

York palmed himself, raking his hand over his silken flesh from root to tip. "I hear that human men are not as well-endowed."

Cassidy shook her head. "Nowhere near — "

His eyes dropped back to her chest as he toed off his boots. "You have the most stunning mammary glands I have ever seen." Her boobs were slightly bigger than the average woman's, but they really weren't all that perky any more. Gravity was a bitch. They were okay at best, yet, you wouldn't say it by the look on York's handsome face. He looked like he had lost his ability to think.

Cassidy giggled and had to put a hand over her mouth to stifle a laugh when he almost fell on his face as he tried to step out of his pants. His eyes were so glued to her chest that he wasn't concentrating on the job at hand. It was really cute. He had a huge grin on his face when he locked eyes with her after righting himself.

"You can touch them if you want." She pushed out her chest.

The grin instantly became a thin white line as he pursed his lips. "I would like nothing more." Low and gravelly, his voice was deeper than any man's that she had ever met. It made goosebumps break out all over her body.

Her nipples tightened as his large calloused hands closed over her boobs. His skin was really warm. He squeezed them a couple of times. "So soft," he whispered, his eyes wide. Then he raked his thumbs over her nipples and she moaned. "You like that?"

She nodded, groaning louder when he gave them both a light pinch. "Very much." Her voice sounded breathless… needy.

York leaned down and sucked on one of her taut nubs. Nipping and sucking intermittently until she was squirming. It felt like she might come from just his mouth on her breast. He squeezed her other breast, still seeming in awe of them. By the time he released her, she was so wet that she could feel the slickness between her legs leaking onto her inner thigh. She felt a little embarrassed. This had never happened to her before. Her and Sean had kept lube in the side table next to their bed because she struggled to get wet enough to take him.

It was like she had turned into a sex kitten.

Maybe the problem had never been hers in the first place. The thought was sobering.

"Get on the bed," he instructed, his eyes locked with hers.

Cassidy did as he said, lying down in the middle of the mattress.

"Open your legs for me." He stepped forward so that he was standing right on the edge of the bed.

Although she felt completely mortified, she did as

he said.

"Wider, Cassidy. I want to look at you before I fuck you with my tongue."

That sent shivers racing up and down her spine. It had her clit throbbing double time.

She sucked in a rugged breath. "Okay," she whispered, doing as he asked. Heat crept over her whole body.

York stared down at her. His nostrils flared. His muscles bunched. He looked like he was doing everything in his power to keep from pouncing on her. "Where is your fur?"

"My what?" *Unexpected.* She wasn't sure what he was talking about.

"Where is your pussy fur?" he whispered, looking her in the eye.

"My hair—" She made a croaky noise out of sheer embarrassment. This was not usual bedroom conversation. "Um... I had it waxed off."

"What is waxed?" His brow furrowed.

"I remove it every couple of weeks. Is that a problem?" she asked, having to fight the urge to close her legs.

"No problem," he murmured, giving her a half-smile. "We were briefed that human females have fur... hair on their pussies and I was just curious. I think your pussy is stunning! So damned wet..." It was all the warning she got. One moment he was standing at the foot of the bed and the next he was between her legs, his tongue buried deep inside of her.

Tongue fucking.

Now there was a concept. The guy was well versed

in the art. He knew where her sweet spot was and laid into it like this was his last supper. Her back came off the bed and her eyes opened wide in her skull before she closed them tight. It took everything in her not to cry out, moan... something. Sean didn't like going down on her, so this was one hell of a treat. The only time she had ever had an orgasm was on the few occasions early on in their relationship when he had used his mouth on her. It wasn't like this though. Not nearly as intense.

York knew exactly what he was doing. From the sounds he was making, he was enjoying himself too. His tongue made lapping, sucking noises. Low little growls seemed to escape every so often as well. Then he slipped his tongue out of her and laved her entire slit. Even licked her inner thigh. "Fuck, you taste so good." His glowing eyes flashed to her. His gaze stayed on her for a few beats. Then he smiled. "No screaming, Cassidy."

Then he was back between her legs where he zeroed in on her clit. Using circular motions with his tongue, he kept at the bundle of nerves until she had to throw her head back. Biting back a moan, she grabbed his head pulling him in closer as she felt the build, felt the tightening of the many coils deep inside her. Everything felt interconnected. Her muscles began to tense.

It was so much more intense with someone else administering the pleasure than when she had done it herself. Suddenly, one year felt like a very long time. York gave a soft nip at her flesh and then sucked her clit hard. She clenched her teeth as her orgasm rushed through her. She couldn't help it when a low groan escaped. Her legs vibrated with the extreme pleasure that shattered her from the inside out. When she finally came down, she realized that she had his head squeezed between her thighs, that her hand held him against her, her nails were digging into his scalp. "Oh… I'm sorry. I guess I got carried away." She released him.

"You can squeeze me between your lush thighs anytime, gorgeous." He licked his lips. "I will give you a few minutes to recover…" His eyes dipped back to between her legs. "I'm still really hungry."

"Um…" She wasn't really much of an aggressor in bed but she really wanted to give a little loving back to York. It was only fair. "Lie down on your back."

York frowned, but did as she said. "What did you have in mind?"

"I'm going to give you a blowjob." She slid her hand around his impressive shaft. It was so thick that her fingers couldn't touch. She slid her hand up and down, marveling at the soft, silky texture. It was a monster of a dick but a rather pretty, velvet covered monster.

York hissed and rocked his hips as she continued to tug on him. Oh god, the thrust move he made was expert. She could just imagine how it would feel having him thrusting deep inside of her like that. Good thing there was a contract or she'd be tempted to try and see if he could fit.

"Are you going to suck on me?" His eyes were wide. His huge chest moved fast.

Wait a minute. He looked like… no way. "Have you never had a blowjob before?"

York shook his head. "Vampire females have sharp fangs."

"Well then hold on, big boy." Cassidy couldn't help but grin. She knew she was good at this. Sean was not big on compliments, but he had told her, on more than one occasion that she gave the best head. It made her sick to her stomach just thinking about exactly what that meant. *Not going there. Not right now.* Cassidy leaned down and took the head of his cock into her mouth.

York cursed... loudly.

It made Cassidy giggle softly. "You need to keep quiet."

York grinned at her. His skin was taut. "That felt really good. I'm more prepared this time."

She dipped her head down

"Cassidy," he stopped her, just as her lips were about to close on him.

"Yeah?" She looked up.

"Make sure that you don't swallow or get any of my come on you." His eyes were serious. They darkened up. "They will be able to scent me on you tomorrow if you do. I'll tell you when I'm about to come."

She nodded, dipping back down. "And, Cassidy..."

"Yeah?" She licked her lips.

"Thank you for doing this for me." Sincerity shone in his eyes.

She almost felt like crying. It was one of the nicest things anyone had ever said to her. Cassidy nodded. She was going to make damned sure that this was the best blowjob he ever had. She looked back down at his bulbous head. It was really big. As she was about to take him into her mouth, his dick twitched in her hand, a drop of pre-cum beaded at the top. She smiled, knowing how aroused he must be. Cassidy lifted her gaze to York who was looking down at her. He had a pained expression on his handsome face. Little indents appeared on his full bottom lip as he bit down on it.

First, she licked her lips, then she licked around the rim of his cock. His mouth turned slack and he made a soft, pained noise. Then she sucked on his head, enjoying the taste of him on her tongue. Salty, with just a hint of sweetness. York's head dropped backwards for a few seconds before his eyes locked back with hers. His breathing was ragged. Cassidy didn't know exactly why but she loved that she was the first ever to give him head. This big powerful vampire had never experienced this before. It was heady.

She continued to suck on his head for a few beats before taking him into her mouth – as deep as he would go. She used her hand in a slow, up and down motion on the base of his shaft. York cursed softly. His eyes glowed even brighter. His hands were fisted at his sides. He was in a crunch position that showcased his abs to perfection. She was tempted to put her hand out and run it over them. So damned pretty – in a badass way of course.

Sure to keep the suction on him just right, not too hard and not too soft, she opened her throat and took him deeper. Fighting the gag reflex in a big way. It was worth it. She watched as his eyes widened, as his mouth widened so that he could suck in more air. His hands clawed the sheets. "Whatever you do, don't stop," he moaned. "You are so fucking beautiful."

Another deep growl. "I love your mouth on me." He clenched his teeth as she deep-throated him again.

"I'm not going to last..." Sweat beaded on his brow. She picked up the pace, alternating between sucking on his head and taking him down her throat.

Within a half a minute she felt his hand stroke the top of her head. "I'm going to—" he groaned pushing her away.

Cassidy moved quickly. Their eyes were still locked as he grabbed his cock, pumping it with his fist in hard, even strokes. The other hand was closed over his tip. She watched as his eyes glazed over. Every muscle corded and he crunched forward. His teeth were clenched as he groaned softly. Most of his come squirted into his hand but some dripped onto his stomach. York fell back, chest heaving. "I just need half a minute to recover."

Disappointment hit. Then he would leave. She didn't want him to leave just yet. "Take your time," she whispered.

York smiled at her. "Let me clean up this mess. I'll be back in a second."

"Here, take a few of these." She grabbed a few tissues from her bag at the side of the bed.

"Yeah, we wouldn't want any accidents. No one must find out I was here." He grabbed the tissues and used them to clean the worst of the mess before pushing them against his member and heading for the bathroom.

Holy hell!

His butt was amazing. Made for grabbing during hot sex. It was well-muscled and sculpted to perfection. Why did the hottest, sweetest guy she'd ever met have to be an off-limits vampire? *Why?* Why was she even thinking of him in terms of a boyfriend? Maybe because she didn't have random sex. The thought of what she had just done made her feel a little light-headed.

She also suddenly felt naked and wrapped a blanket around herself. There was the sound of running water followed by the toilet flushing. York came back into the room. Oh wow, he was still semi-erect.

York gave her a mischievous half-smile, he'd probably noticed her checking out his junk. Instead of getting dressed like she expected, he slid into bed next to her and pulled her into his arms.

What!

Why?

She had to bite down on her lip when he removed the blanket so that she was flush against his side. Skin to skin. It didn't mean anything. He was probably vying for another blowjob or something.

"You seem a little tense. Do you need me to — "

"No!" It came out a little too harshly. "I mean... um... it's just that we don't know each other and this feels a little awkward all of a sudden. It's not you or anything... I don't normally do things like this."

His chest vibrated as he chuckled softly. "Tell me something about yourself then. Maybe it would make you feel better."

She shrugged. "I don't know what to say. I'm nearly thirty..." She smiled. "Next month, I'll hit the big three-zero."

"Why are you not mated? Am I right in saying that

most human females are settled by thirty?"

Her first instinct was to bristle at his words but then she realized that he was just being his normal honest, forward self and she took a deep breath instead.

"Why do my questions anger you?" Maybe he didn't know that he was doing it, but he began to stroke her back. His big, warm hands felt good on her even though they shouldn't. Maybe it was because it had been so long since someone had touched her like this.

Cassidy shrugged. "I don't know. I guess because I thought I would be married – mated – at thirty. I was married but..." She let the sentence die.

His arms tightened around her for a second before he released his hold. She could feel how tense he had become. "I had heard that humans sometimes take several mates throughout their lives. It is hard for us vampires to understand. Were you not happy with your chosen mate?" he sounded angry.

This time she did allow herself to feel pissed at his words and pulled away. "My husband died, so you can stop looking at me like I'm something the cat dragged in."

"I'm not sure what a cat has to do with it," he muttered. "I'm so damned sorry." He hauled her back into his arms, pulling her tight against him. One of his hands cupped the side of her head while the other curled around her waist. He hugged her tight, burying his head into her hair for a while. "That can't have been easy. No wonder this has been difficult for you. I'm so sorry." He rubbed her back. This time with harder strokes designed more to soothe than to pleasure.

Her eyes filled with tears. York really seemed to care. His voice sounded rough with emotion. He was really sorry for what he had said. "It's okay."

"No it's not." He pulled her away from him so that he could look at her. "I'm a serious dick for thinking the worst of you. I'm sorry!" He cursed. "You're crying."

"I'm not crying," she sniffed. Her eyes might be filled with tears but none had spilled over yet so technically she wasn't crying.

His eyes narrowed. "You are." Using his thumb, he rubbed at the moisture that had gathered at the edge of her eye. "You must have really loved him. I can't imagine how much you must miss him."

As in, not so much.

"Stop. Please."

York shook his head. "It hurts too much to talk of him... I understand."

"No, it's not that. You're wrong. Totally off base." It just slipped out.

"*Wrong?* What do mean by that?" he frowned.

The can of worms was already open, might as well let those suckers run free. "In hindsight my relationship with Sean, my husband, was not all that great. We were just going through the motions as a married couple. We didn't have the best sexual relationship... we didn't have the best relationship period. I just didn't see it at the time." She took a deep breath. "I found out some things after his death that made me realize that I didn't know him nearly as well as I had always thought. I don't miss him... not one tiny bit."

York was frowning. "What did you find out?"

"You really don't want to know. No one knows about it and I'd rather it stayed that way." She bit down on her lower lip, hoping he would leave it alone.

"I do want to know," he whispered. "I really think you should tell me. I can see that you need to talk. You can't let whatever it is stay inside you like this. I promise not to tell another living soul." He touched his heart and she was oddly affected by the gesture.

"I found some receipts after his death. It turned out that Sean had a little gambling problem. Not only did he clean out our savings account, he also maxed out three credit cards. I'm buried under a ton of debt."

Although York's eyes darkened and his jaw tensed, he didn't say anything.

After a long minute, she carried on. "I worked out that if I lived on beans, it would take me five years to pay it off at my current rate of pay. That's why I'm here. I need a fresh start. I really need the money." Her mind went to the credit card statements and phone text messages she had found and the feeling of betrayal hit her all over again like it had happened just yesterday.

"There's more." York took ahold of her hand and squeezed. "You can trust me with this."

Cassidy licked her lips and nodded. "I had a long look at the credit card statements. I was trying so hard to decipher where all the money had gone. Trying to understand what Sean had been thinking. I suspected that there was more. It turned out that he had used the cards every week at a local club called 'The Kitten's

Paws.' It was a standard two hundred dollar deduction every Thursday afternoon at around his lunch break. It made me curious so I went to check it out." Her lip wobbled as she remembered the utter horror she had felt at her discovery. "The Kitten's Paw is an escort agency. A really dirty, dingy one at that. After checking his cell phone, I found that he messaged one of his hookers every week to confirm their appointment. He bounced between three or four girls at the club." She scrubbed a hand over her face.

"Forgive me." York sounded unsure. "What is an escort agency? I am also not familiar with the term hooker." His eyebrows drew together under his deep frown.

"He was paying a woman every week to have sex with him."

"Why the fuck would he do that?"

She had to laugh at his response. "Why do men do the things that they do? Not only men; women can be just as bad."

"He had you warming his bed yet he paid money to rut someone else?" York shook his head. He looked both shocked and disgusted. "What an idiot."

His words warmed her.

"I can tell you right now that if you were mine, I wouldn't need anyone else." A rumbling whisper so sincere that it had her holding her breath for a few seconds.

"Thank you," it slipped out before she could stop it. It made her sound really pathetic.

"Why are you thanking me?" York looked confused.

"I don't know…" She felt embarrassed to admit that he treated her better than any man ever had. Certainly better than Sean ever treated her.

York squeezed her hand. "You had better not be thanking me for what I just said." His eyes travelled the length of her. "You are a sexy female, Cassidy. I should be thanking you and not the other way around."

She couldn't help but smile, having to avert her eyes while she pulled herself together. "I can say thank you if I want to… you're really sweet. I also want to thank you for the orgasm. It's been a very long time since I had one and…" She bit down on her bottom lip. Her confidence, suddenly waning. "I enjoyed it very much," she managed to squeak out the last, while hoping to god that she didn't sound like a loser.

"How long has your poor excuse for a mate been dead?" His frown deepened and he actually looked angry when talking about Sean. It was probably just her imagination.

"Almost a year now. He died a few days after my birthday in a car accident."

"A year is a very long time to go without coming." His eyes were wide and his eyebrows were raised.

"It's been a damn sight longer than a year," she blurted, instantly regretting her big mouth. She wasn't normally like this. There was something about York's direct nature that brought the same out in her.

He frowned. "I thought you said your mate died a year ago?"

She pulled on a loose piece of thread on the blanket. "I also said that we didn't have the best sexual relationship."

York sat upright, dragging her with him. "Are you telling me that, not only did your dickhead mate screw other females but he didn't take care of you either? That he didn't ensure that your needs were met?"

"You're being too loud... we're going to get busted."

York cursed beneath his breath. "I'm sorry. It's just that hearing about your relationship with him makes me really pissed. I know that it is wrong to speak badly of the dead but I think he was an idiot and a jerk. That he would rut other women but not with his own female just fucks me off."

"We used to have sex at least once a week... it's just that... well... he never made me... you know... come," she mumbled the last word, heat creeping up her cheeks. "As in, not one time... ever."

"You've never had an orgasm during sex? Is that what you are telling me?" Not only was his jaw clenched but a muscle ticked as well.

She shook her head, feeling mortified. Her face felt hot. Why was she telling him all of this?

York slid out of bed. Did knowing that she couldn't have a g-spot orgasm turn him off? His dick was fully erect. It jutted from his body. So that didn't seem like a reasonable explanation. He paced up and down twice before running a hand over his scalp.

Cassidy pulled the blanket around herself. "Why are you so angry?"

York returned to the bed, crouching down so that she would hear him. "It's unacceptable that you have never had an orgasm during sex. How long were you mated?"

"Four years."

His eyes rolled back in anger. They came back blazing. "Four years and you never came once?"

She shook her head. "He went down on me a few times after we first got married which was when I did orgasm but he didn't like doing it."

His jaw worked but he didn't say anything.

Cassidy shrugged. "He called it carpet munching and often joked, saying that he wasn't a damned vacuum cleaner. I guess that's why I started waxing in the first place. Why am I telling you all of this? I don't even know you."

He smiled at her. "What you see is what you get. You know me well enough." He rose to his feet. "Where is it?"

She felt herself frown. "What?"

"The contract that you signed. Please tell me you have a copy."

7

HER STUNNING GREEN-TINGED eyes tracked him as he rose to his feet. An adorable frown took up residence on her face. "Why do you need the contract?"

"I want to take a look at that no sex clause. There has to be a way around it."

Her frown deepened and she chewed on her full bottom lip, making him want a taste. This female was utter perfection. From her golden, honey-infused skin to the soft smattering of freckles that spilled over her nose onto her cheeks. "What do you mean? Why do you need to find a way around the clause?" Her chest rose and fell quickly, telling him that she knew the answer to that question.

Cassidy shook her head, pulling the blanket more closely around herself. It made him want to rip it from her. Curves like that should never be covered. Not ever.

York looked at her pointedly, making sure that she

would be able to read his desire for her. "I am going to make you come several times with my dick buried deep inside you. In order to make that happen, we need to find a way around that clause."

Cassidy gasped. Her perfect lips rounded, reminding him of how incredible they had looked wrapped around his cock. It was a sight he would never tire of. One that he would think of often.

Her eyes flashed with anger. "I told you that I don't need any pity orgasms. Thanks for everything but I think you should go now." She suddenly looked sad. It made his gut churn.

York gave a humorless chuckle. It came out sounding weird because he was still whispering. "I'm a selfish bastard, Cassidy. Do I want to feel you shudder underneath me as you come...really hard? Yes I do. Do I want to be the first male who brings that kind of pleasure to you using only my dick? Abso-fucking-lutely. But please don't be mistaken... I want to feel my own release just as badly. I want to feel your tight pussy wrapped around me. Moreover, I want to feel you grow ever fucking tighter as you come all over my dick and I don't think I can let you go until I have. It would be just as much about me as it would be about you. Am I clear?"

Way to go, York. Talk about scaring a timid human away.

Her eyes flared and her mouth rounded out even more. Then the delicious scent of her arousal enveloped him and she swallowed hard. He was fucked if she wasn't turned on right now. Not as timid as he thought. Damned if it didn't make him harder for her.

Cassidy licked her lips and for a second time he was mesmerized as the little pink tip swept across her lips in a slow glide that made him bite back a moan.

"It's in the top drawer of the dresser."

She was some female and he had to have her.

Had. To.

One way or another. If there wasn't a way around the clause, he would pay her out himself. York didn't care about money. The coven was wealthy, which meant that he was wealthy. He would make sure that she received her payout fair and square. He meant what he had said, there was no way he could watch her walk away without having had her. He wasn't lying when he said that he was self-centered. In this, he was a selfish prick but this female had made him momentarily insane. At least, that's what it felt like.

York pulled out the thick, heavy document.

It would take at least an hour to read through each and every clause. *Screw that!* He tossed it back in the drawer. "Do you trust me?"

She nodded without hesitation and he felt something strange inside his chest. It was more than likely pride... yeah that's what it was, pride that even after all that had happened she trusted him. He would not fail her. "Good," he assured her. "I guarantee that you will be paid out in full regardless of what happens. I will take the fall for this." He put his hand against his chest. "You're here for the money, right?"

Cassidy nodded.

"Please trust me that you will get your cash even if you are booted tomorrow." He put a knee on the bed and sat down next to her.

"How can you be so sure?" Her eyes were on his dick while she spoke but they soon lifted to lock with his.

"I'm head of the elite team. Number one." He wasn't one for bragging but he had to make her understand that he did have some pull within the covens. Brant would serve him his ass but quite frankly he didn't give a shit. One night with this female would be worth it. The bastard hadn't listened to him earlier. Cassidy would get her money and everyone would be happy.

Except he was out. No longer one of the ten. There was a painful clench deep inside him. Chances were good that he would never be a father. It was something he would worry about tomorrow.

"I promise you, that you will be paid out in full regardless of what happens. I'm not going to lie to you, there will be hell to pay in the morning but I'll take the brunt of it."

"Why though? Surely you could have anyone?" Her cheeks immediately flushed scarlet. He could see that she hadn't meant to say that.

"I don't want just anyone. I want you, Cassidy."

She gave a shake of her head and her mouth curled up at the corners. "You don't even know me."

York found himself smiling back. "I know you well enough. Like I said before, we're drawn together on a physical level… you can't deny it."

She licked her lips but didn't respond. York could see that she was having an internal war.

"Answer me one thing…"

Nodding, the blanket slipped off of one shoulder giving him an unobstructed view of the top of one of her rounded breasts. Cassidy had the best mammary glands he had ever seen on a female. Lush, weighty… so soft that his hands itched to touch them again.

He cleared his throat when he realized that she was waiting for him to continue. With a small shake of the head, she gave him a knowing smile. Thankfully she looked amused rather than angry after the eyeball fuck he had just given her. "Right," he whispered. "Where was I?" he grinned.

"I needed to answer you one thing." She raised her brows, looking so utterly fuckable it was scary.

York gave a deep nod. "Do you want me to fuck you right now?" He lifted his hand as he watched her face cloud in thought. She was over-thinking the hell out of it.

"Don't think of consequences or any of that. You said that you were here for the money and you're scared of being chucked out of the trial phase if we do this."

She nodded.

"I've already guaranteed that you will be paid so what's stopping you?"

"Nothing I guess. Thing is, I don't normally do things like this. It would just be this once, right?"

York hesitated before answering. He would've liked to have had more with her. Shit, she was everything he'd ever wanted in a female. It would be great to explore this attraction. Maybe there was something deeper there. It could never happen though. Even if by some miracle he was allowed back into the program, the human females had already been selected based on strict criteria. Cassidy was not one of them. "Yes…" His voice sounded odd so he cleared his throat. "Just tonight." He was done trying to convince her. "Your choice, Cassidy. I will respect your decision either way." He shut his mouth and waited for her to think about it.

For a second, he was sure that she looked disappointed but she quickly schooled her expression. "Okay then. I think I would regret it if I didn't."

"You don't have to sound so enthusiastic about it," he had to chuckle. "You really don't have to do this." He had to make sure that she really wanted this, that she wouldn't have regrets in the morning.

She smiled. "I'm sure."

York let out a breath that he didn't even know he was holding. He'd never had to work so hard to get a female into his bed. The vampire females knew his position in the coven. He normally had his pick. This whole concept of having to work for it was foreign to him… he liked it.

With a small shrug of the shoulder, Cassidy let the blanket fall in a puddle around her. He had to clench his teeth to keep from snarling. Her beauty called to him in a primal way. She looked up at him from under long black lashes. Her equally dark hair had become a wild tangle about her shoulders from their earlier tussle. Her eyes were big, with an innocent quality that brought out the protector in him.

Her breasts had his dick throbbing between his thighs. She hadn't had sex in a long time and she had never had a vampire before, so things would be tight down there. He knew that to be true from the way her pussy had hugged his tongue earlier and his dick was a damn sight bigger.

As much as he wanted to turn her over and pound into her warm flesh, he was going to take his time and make this about her. Round two could be hard and fast – but still about her.

York moved over to Cassidy and kissed her softly, keeping his hands at his sides. They had been instructed during training that human females enjoyed the act of touching of the lips and the tangling of the tongues. He had kissed before, although not often. Rutting was about release; kissing, in his opinion, did nothing to bring about that end. Yet, with Cassidy, he found that he enjoyed it. It was like a mating of the tongues. He liked how her hot breath mingled with his. How her breathless panting very quickly turned choppy. *Damn, but he could drown in her taste.* If sunshine and rainbows had a flavor, then this was it. York cupped her chin deepening their kiss, swallowing her whimper and demanding that she give him more.

He pulled her onto his lap and she straddled him while linking her arms around his neck. York put a hand to her pussy and had to break the kiss so that he could groan. "You're still so wet, Cassidy." Keeping his eyes on hers, he breached her opening with a single finger.

Her mouth fell open and her eyes heated up. York pushed deeper into her channel, loving the feel of her slick heat.

Cassidy licked her lips, panting softly as he began

to finger fuck her. "Oh god, that feels good," she whimpered. "I can't believe it... and it's just your finger."

He kissed the tip of her cute nose before taking back her mouth. Sliding two fingers inside her, he kept thrusting into her using easy strokes. Cassidy moaned and he ate up the sound. She was rocking against his hand. One more finger – he had to prepare her for his thick girth. Her moan erupted and she slapped a hand over her mouth. "I didn't know it could feel this good." A hoarse whisper that had his dick twitching between them.

"You haven't felt anything yet, gorgeous." He withdrew his fingers and she moaned in frustration. "Are you ready for me?"

Her eyes widened. "Are you sure you'll fit?"

York trailed soft kisses along her collarbone using one of his hands to knead her spectacular mammary glands. "There's only one way to find out." He would fucking die if he didn't fit.

"Um... okay." Then she sucked in a ragged breath. "What about protection?"

"You're not in heat so no risk of pregnancy and I can't give you any human illnesses since I don't get them." He softly pinched one of her nipples and she moaned. Using the same hand, he found her clit and stroked it.

Cassidy's eyes opened really wide and she clamped her mouth shut. "It's hard to think when you're doing that."

"The time for thinking is over. I'm going to fuck you now, Cassidy." He tried to keep the desperation out of his voice. "Feel free to kiss me – or bite me – if you feel like screaming."

Her head looked too heavy for her neck and she was panting hard. Her eyes were at half-mast. In short, she was really close to orgasm which was exactly where he wanted her.

York took ahold of her hips and lifted her so that his cock lined up with her opening. "You need to do this, Cassidy, ease yourself onto me."

She nodded, putting her hand between them. He hissed out a breath as her little fingers closed on him. "You are so big." Awe mingled with fear.

"My cock will touch every nerve-ending inside of you. Sit on me, Cass, take it slow."

She nodded, pushing onto his head. They both groaned as he breached her tight opening. "Oh god." She was panting – big time. "That stings."

Using one hand to hold her up, he pushed the other between their bodies quickly finding her clit. He used soft strokes designed to make her feel good rather than to make her come. He didn't want her over the edge just yet, he wanted to keep her wet and heavily aroused.

She pushed down onto him and he sank in an inch. Her eyes were closed. Her mouth became a thin white line.

"Cass, we don't have to…" It would kill him but he could stop. He hated to see her face lined with pain.

"I want to." She slid down another inch.

She was squeezing him so damned tight that he could hardly breathe. York slid out of her and pushed back in. In and out. Staying shallow. He kept up the slip and slide over her clit. "Are you okay?" he managed to grind out.

Cassidy nodded. "I want more."

Fucking music to his ears. He pushed back in giving her another inch. Her mouth fell open and her eyes widened. In and out... this time pushing in to the new depth.

Cassidy moaned softly. She licked her lush lips. "I'm ready for more."

This went on for a few minutes, until he finally felt her ass against him. She gave him a tight smile, her cheeks were flushed and her eyes glassy with desire. "You fit."

"Don't sound so shocked." He nipped her bottom lip and she nipped him back, sucking his lip into her mouth.

Damn, if it wasn't one of the sexiest things a female had ever done to him.

"You can fuck me now." A breathy whisper that almost had him coming.

His balls were already in his throat. His skin felt tight. Everything in him was tight and ready.

"I want my orgasm." She nipped at his lip and he lost his ability to think as he began to move.

Her eyes rolled back on the first hard thrust. It was like someone had thrown a bucket of ice water over him. He tightened his hold. "Fuck, Cassidy, did I hurt you?"

"Don't stop... don't you dare stop." Her eyes were blazing with anger and desire in equal measures.

York's chuckle died as he picked up where he had left off. So hot, so wet, so tight he was sure his dick wasn't getting any blood supply. Even though her mouth was clenched, she was making loud whimpering noises. He knew the guards downstairs might hear and there would be no doubt as to what was happening upstairs, so he kissed her. Their tongues warring in a hot, rhythmic embrace, much the same as their bodies. He could feel the sweat on his brow. Could feel his body beg for release. His balls throbbed. His dick throbbed. His body vibrated with the need. Instead of giving in as he wanted – downright needed – he continued to thrust.

Her pussy walls quivered, her arms tightened around his neck, her fingers dug into his shoulders. Then her channel tightened around him. It was impossible not to come, and hard. His fangs erupted, forcing him to break their kiss. The last thing he wanted was to hurt her. Cassidy buried her head in his neck and bit him. Harder than before. Maybe even hard enough to draw blood because his dick erupted all over again, his orgasm spiraling out of control.

He had to fight the urge to bite her back, going against every instinct in him. If he bit Cassidy, she would scream and alert the guards. He wasn't done with her yet. Not nearly. She thankfully released her hold on his neck, allowing him to find some semblance of control, to slow his thrusting.

Both were breathing so hard that he was afraid that the assholes downstairs would hear even that, but no one came. Cassidy put her head against his chest. He could feel how heavy she felt in his arms. York had to smile. He had made her this way. A completely sated, boneless heap of loveliness.

"Oh wow," she finally sighed.

Her breasts were mashed against his chest. He could feel her panting against his skin. It really wasn't his fault when his dick hardened back up again. He was still buried deep inside her. Cassidy pulled away from him. She choked out a silent laugh, her eyes wide. "You're kidding me."

"I told you that you make me hard and I don't lie," he whispered back.

Damned if her eyes didn't turn a little wicked, if she didn't give him a naughty smile.

"Are you ready for the next round, Cass?" he asked. "I don't plan on going easy on you this time."

Her lower lip disappeared between her teeth and her breathing became a little labored. She nodded. "Definitely."

"Good. Have you ever rutted doggy style?" It was a position guaranteed to hit the g-spot. He would have her seeing stars in no time.

It was a rhetorical question so when Cassidy shook her head, it had him vibrating with anger. What the hell had been wrong with her mate? He refrained from saying anything but only because the asshole had passed and it would be wrong to speak badly of the dead. To not have ever experienced doggy style was a sin… a travesty.

"We only made love in the missionary position." She looked away from him for a few seconds. "Sex was pretty boring and over in minutes." She must've caught his pissed look because she quickly added. "I also blame myself, I never offered to try anything new or to wear any sexy lingerie or anything."

With extreme reluctance, York pulled out of Cassidy for the moment. She was confiding in him again. Something he knew she didn't do often. It made him feel good to know that she trusted him with her secrets. With the things that he could tell had been on her mind for some time.

"Lingerie?" He repeated the word, no clue as to what she was talking about. They had been warned that although vampires and humans were highly compatible, they definitely had major differences.

"Human women wear sexy underwear designed to turn a man on. It's called lingerie and is made from lace and ribbon and is normally sheer or will plump up a woman's breasts."

He had to frown. "Underwear..." He shook his head. "Naked is so much better. If you want to entice a vampire, don't wear anything at all. Underwear would just get ripped off."

She laughed and her breasts jiggled making him almost forget what he wanted to say next. "It was not your fault. You are a highly sensual female. It is up to the male to make an effort... to keep his female satisfied."

She gave him a look that told him she thought he was full of it.

"I'm serious. There was no pay off for you so you didn't put in much effort. That's not wrong on your part."

Her gaze moved to somewhere just north of his head before locking back with his. "You're right. I married Sean because he was a good friend. We got along really well. He did make more of an effort in the early days." She paused for a time. "We didn't have the greatest marriage, I can see that now. It didn't give him the right to do the things that he did though. I had to go and get myself tested after I found out about 'The Kitty's Paw.' It was one of the hardest things I have ever had to do." Her eyes clouded in pain. "I was so relieved when the tests came back clean. I hated him so much in that moment. He was my best friend and he betrayed my trust. I thought I knew him but I didn't."

His muscles tensed. If the guy was still breathing, York would find him and punch him. There was no honor in his actions.

"I don't want to talk about it anymore. What about you? I've told you so much about my life and I know nothing about you."

York shrugged. "I told you that I head up the Elite team. I am in charge of ensuring the safety of our kings, as well as the queen and of course our heir."

"Yeah, that made headlines in the local paper last week. The paparazzi are camped outside the front gates in the hopes of getting the first picture of the little one. There is so much speculation as to the sex of the child. It's all very exciting."

York felt a warmth rise up inside him at the thought of the baby. So small and innocent, from his chubby little cheeks to his tiny little hands. "The baby is a boy, his name is Sam – after the queen's younger brother who died when he was just three. He is the cutest little guy."

Her eyes widened and then she smiled. "Isn't that classified information?"

He shrugged. "You trusted me and now I'm trusting you."

Her smile widened. "Thank you. I won't tell... I promise."

York dragged a thumb down the side of her face, loving the soft feel of her skin. This female was a vision. He was just getting ready to kiss her again, to feel her pliable lips against his – to do a whole lot more – when she cocked her head. "So, did you choose to be enrolled in the program or was it mandatory?"

It was crazy, he'd waited months for the program to kick off. He should've been working on a plan to get back into it right at that moment. Trying to figure out a way to change Brant's mind and to prove to him that he didn't have bloodlust. Yet, right then, he didn't give a damn about any of that. He only cared about the female in his arms. He saw it for what it was, lust, plain and simple, but it rode him harder than ever before.

He didn't want to talk anymore but he answered her anyway. "It's not mandatory. We had to fight our way in. The top ten fighters were awarded positions."

"Let me guess..." Her eyes were bright. "You had to have been one of the top three?"

York couldn't help but to laugh softly. "So little faith. I told you, I'm number one. I was the last elite standing."

"Arrogant much?" she teased, but he could see that she didn't mean it.

"Actually, yes. I fight hard for what I want." He growled and pulled her closer to him.

"And what is it that you want?" Her whole demeanor changed. Cassidy seemed to hold her breath. Seemed to really care about his answer. Although her question had sounded flirty, she was being serious. She genuinely wanted to know what made him tick.

At first he thought of giving her a flippant answer but he couldn't, not after she had just bared her soul. "I really want a family... children. A female to love who will love me back. Hot, sexy nights and fun-filled days. I want the sound of children's laughter to fill my home." York took a deep breath realizing that he had gone off on a bit of a tangent. Said more than he had planned.

When he focused back on Cassidy, her eyes had a faraway look. There was a definite look of longing on her beautiful face. Her normally bright eyes turned murky, flashing with pain that tore at him.

Then she smiled and it was gone. "Wow... I'm sure you'll get it in the end. Maybe Brant will give you a second chance. If anyone can convince him, it's you."

He shrugged. "Maybe. I don't want to think about it right now. That's something to worry about tomorrow. Right now..." He could feel how his fangs ached in his gums. Longing for a taste. His eyes even drifted to the pulse at the base of her neck. Two pairs of small red marks marred her perfect honey soaked skin. There would be no biting. "Get onto your knees, Cass."

She did as he asked, giving him a perfect view of her stunning ass and her glistening pussy.

"Grab a pillow to stifle your cries," he instructed, a sense of urgency clawed at him.

Swallowing thickly, she did as he said, the scent of

her arousal filled the room. Cassidy was his for tonight and he planned on making the most of it. For whatever reason, it was important to him that she never forgot him or their time together.

So this was what it felt like to be treated like a criminal. Guards flanked him on all sides. He was outnumbered, so it wouldn't help to try to fight his way out. Except for Gideon, the males were not from his elite team, so it wouldn't help to try to talk his way out either.

York had purposefully turned up before breakfast in an effort to see Brant before Cassidy left her room anyhow. Once the vampire guards caught her scent they would know exactly what had gone down. That was why he was here in the first place. To sort shit out before it became Cassidy's problem.

By then, he wanted everything out in the open. The ass-whipping he was about to receive would be long over.

They kept moving, the guards were leading him into the belly of the castle. Gideon's jaw was set, he walked on ahead of the formation. "Fucking insanity," he muttered as they rounded the last turn. The male pulled open a door and gestured for him to enter. "Good luck," he muttered softly as York was about to enter the room. There was a ghost of a smile playing about Gideon's lips. If he didn't know better, he would say that the male was on his side, or at least that he had some sort of understanding for his predicament. Gideon had been promoted to head of security for the breeding program. He was the most straight and narrow, controlled, reliable vampire he knew. It didn't make any sense that he would have any understanding. York had broken some serious rules and crossed some serious lines. Gideon never put a foot wrong... not ever.

"Get your ass in there," Gideon barked.

York realized that he had been staring at the other male.

Both Brant and Zane sat at the same side of a long mahogany table. They both had their arms folded across their chests and they both looked pissed. Brant's hair was mussed, when he ran a hand through the unruly mess, York realized why that was.

"You had better have a good explanation." Brant's eyes blazed and his jaw ticked.

York folded his arms in front of him, he didn't even try to take a seat.

"If you say that you tripped and fell and your dick happened to slide into her pussy, I might just kill you with my bare hands." Zane sounded and looked the picture of calm. It made York distinctly uncomfortable.

York shook his head. "I went over there to apologize. I hadn't planned on rutting... or even on touching the female, for that matter."

"Last I heard," Zane's eyes darkened, "you didn't need a dick to apologize. You could've just said the words and left."

Brant leant forward. "Firstly, I told you to stay the fuck away from her and secondly, I told you to stay in your room which indirectly meant to stay the fuck away from her. What part of that didn't you understand?"

"I didn't agree with the part where you told me I had bloodlust. I had upset and terrified the female. I needed to apologize. I'm sorry for disobeying direct orders." He clenched his teeth.

"How did you get out of your room, and more importantly, how did you get to her room without anyone knowing?"

York had to work to keep himself from rolling his eyes. "With all due respect, my lords," he looked at them each in turn, "the guards you posted are a joke. I climbed out my window and walked to the building housing the females. All I had to do was bide my time until the guard moved to the other side of the building. Their movements are predictable. They patrol along the same path at a slow walk. I timed it so that I had thirty seconds to scale the building. The human, Cassidy, had left her window open just a crack…" he shrugged.

"You scaled a three-storey building in thirty seconds using just your hands?" Brant narrowed his eyes, clearly not believing him.

"Yes, my lord. I would be happy to demonstrate. I'm tall and strong… it is my belief that many of the males would be capable. I was almost caught when the female woke up when I pulled her window wider. She got up and went to the bathroom. Thankfully, I had scaled the wall in under thirty seconds and she didn't take too long to leave the room. I was able to enter before the guard made it back to that side of the building."

Brant cursed. He held up a hand while pulling his phone from his pocket. "Get in here."

Gideon entered, standing next to York. The male looked pissed.

"Did you hear that?" Brant asked.

Gideon nodded. "There are holes in our system. I will ensure that they are fixed."

Brant nodded. "You'll need to put guards outside each of the females' rooms. This can't happen again. We need to discuss the night patrols... all the damn patrols for that matter." He glanced at Zane.

Zane leaned back, putting his hands behind his head. "We need to get Sweetwater Security back. I'm thinking motion sensors at all the doors and windows as well as surrounding the building. We also need more cameras... should've known this would happen. I didn't expect it from you." The male smiled. "Then again, if anyone was going to get in and out of that building without anyone being the wiser and then turn themselves in in the morning, it's you." He choked out a laugh.

"This is no laughing matter." Brant looked pointedly at Zane before turning his eyes back to York. "You put my program in jeopardy for a quick fuck. What if it had gone wrong?"

"I didn't go there to rut her. I knew that I didn't have bloodlust so there was no risk. I'm ready for my punishment." He worked hard to keep the anger from his voice. "All I ask is that you leave the female out of it. I talked Cassidy into letting me rut her. It wasn't her fault... she didn't stand a chance against my touches and advances."

"Screw that," Brant snarled. "She signed a contractual agreement and an example needs to be made. She is being sent here as we speak."

Zane chuckled, it turned into a yawn. "All I can say is that you could not have done a very good job if no one heard you with her. I'm disappointed. My top elite warrior doesn't know how to make a female scream. She's a human at that."

York clenched his jaw. He was tempted to tell his king where the hell he could get off. Not because he felt undermined as a male but because he didn't like them talking about Cassidy like she was just a piece of ass. What they had shared may have only been for one night but it was special. She was special and didn't deserve this treatment.

In the end, he ignored Zane and turned to Brant. "I assure you that the female is mostly innocent in this. When a vampire male wants a female – when *I* want a female – *I* get her. Cassidy didn't stand a chance against my advances." He had to try to change Brant's mind about making an example out of her.

There was a knock at the door. "That will be her now," Brant snapped.

Cassidy walked in, she was wearing more of her shapeless clothing. This time it was a loose dress that went to just below the knee, another pair of leg coverings and a buttoned up jacket. She couldn't hide the plump swell of her breasts but you would never know that she hid a gorgeous body underneath those clothes.

Cassidy held her head high.

"Good morning," York grinned at her. He couldn't help himself. It was so good to see her. After they had rutted a third time, Cassidy had fallen into a deep sleep. He didn't have the heart to wake her. York had watched her sleep for a while and then had quietly left through the same window that he came in once the coast was clear.

She gave him a quick half-smile before turning to face Brant and Zane. York noticed that her suitcase was on the ground next to her and her large purse was slung over her shoulder.

Brant breathed in a lungful of air, letting it out slowly. "You will be paid out for yesterday. Last night you were in direct breach of contract when you had sexual relations with York, a vampire male."

Cassidy took a small step forward and licked her lips. "Can I say something please?"

"Don't try to deny it," Brant growled and York was tempted to growl back.

Cassidy didn't even flinch. It made his heart warm just watching her stand up to the male. Brant and Zane were fear-inducing males, even to vampires, let alone to a small, human female.

Cassidy licked her lips again. York could see her visibly square her shoulders and lift her chin a touch higher. She shook her head. "No, York and I had sex," she said matter-of-factly. "Several times in fact."

The tick was back in Brant's jaw.

Cassidy paused for a few beats. "What I wanted to say is that I'm not in breach." She pulled the contract out of her big purse. It was a wonder she could carry the thing, it was so damned big.

"Bull-fucking-shit!" Brant leapt to his feet, knocking his chair so hard it fell to the floor with a crash. "You let York fuck you, that's sexual relations spelled with a capital *S*."

This time York couldn't help himself, He stepped in front of Cassidy and snarled. In that moment, he forgot who he was, and who Brant was. He would've gone at the male if he took even a step towards Cassidy.

Zane rose to his feet. "Let's all calm down." He motioned for the chairs. "Sit." Next he picked up Brant's chair.

His king's eyes had turned a depthless black. "Don't get ahead of yourself, York, or I'll have you tossed in the dungeon for the remainder of the program. You are the Elite Leader, I thought you had a little more control than this."

York had to force air back into his lungs, had to force himself to unclench his fists. Gideon took a seat. Turning, he took in Cassidy's too pale face and shaking hands. York pulled out a chair for her and gestured for her to take a seat.

"Thanks," she whispered, barely looking at him.

"You said you trusted me," he said, not caring about the others in the room. "I meant what I said."

She nodded but her face was still grave. York meant every word.

A booming voice from across the table almost had her wetting her pants.

"If you are not in breach then bacon sandwiches can fly and not only will I let you stay but I'll pay you double every time a vampire drinks from you for the remainder of your stay. You have six sessions scheduled so that's a lot of cash up for grabs." King Brant somehow managed to look bored while speaking. Like there was no way in hell that he was going to lose. It made her feel foolish for even bringing it up.

She wasn't a lawyer. What did she know? For a moment, she was tempted to put the contract away and to leave as quickly and as quietly as possible. The thing was, she and York were both consenting adults. Although she understood why the kings were so pissed, nothing had gone wrong in the end. It had been her risk to take and she would do it again in a heartbeat. Also, she had woken up early and pored over this document. She knew what she had read. She'd gone over it fifty times and looked at it from every angle. According to the contract, she was not in breach. She just had to prove it to the kings.

"The clause specifically states that sexual relations are forbidden during the trial phase of the program." She swallowed thickly. Her mouth felt a bit dry. "It refers to this twice." She looked down at the papers in her hand and at the passage in question. She had underlined those specific parts of the document.

Brant sighed, sounding like he had pretty much had

enough of this whole thing. "We are in the trial phase. That puts you in breach."

"Yeah, but if you refer to the contract document page—" she flipped through the contract several times before she found the right page, "five, Clause 8.1b. Specific Trial phase sessions are referred to." She mentioned the three time slots of half an hour each before turning the page. "On page six... um... clause 10, it mentions that the trial phase will take place in the West block in room A and room B," she went on.

"Look..." Brant sounded irritated. He shoved a hand through his hair. "I've had just about enough of this. Get to the point. As far as I can see, you are in breach. Done freaking deal and enough said. You have even admitted to having sex – several times – with a vampire. You have one minute to make your point or I'm having you physically removed." His eyes were dark and intense. His voice, deep and commanding. For just a second, she was tempted to apologize and be on her way but she knew she was right about this. It wasn't even about the money anymore. King Brant was a dick and she'd had just about enough of him. King Zane wasn't much better since he just sat there yawning every few minutes like he couldn't wait for this to end regardless of who was right and who was wrong.

"I'm not one of your vampires. You can't order me around and treat me like a piece of dirt under your boot. Quite frankly, I don't understand why your people haven't kicked you off your throne and your high horse." *Oops.* She hadn't meant to say that, but quite frankly he deserved it.

His face turned ruby red and his eyes blazed.

Zane burst out laughing. "I like you, human." He turned his gaze to York. "I can see what you saw in her."

"Shut the hell up!" Brant roared.

"We're all ears, human. This had better be good." Zane rose up in his chair and she felt like cowering on the ground in front of him. She turned to face Brant, seeing his hard eyes gave her the push she needed to continue. This asshole needed to be brought down a couple of rungs. It was clear that no one ever stood up to him.

Cassidy licked her lips. *Crunch time.* "York and I had sex in our own personal time. The document specifically refers to no sexual relations during the trial session, it then goes on to define what times trial sessions occur and even gives the location of the trial sessions. I was not in breach. We had sex outside of the trial sessions as specified in here. We weren't anywhere near the building in question." She picked up the document.

Brant's eyes narrowed on her. "Give me the contract." He held out his hand. For a second she was afraid that if she gave it to him he would tear it up. With a shaking hand, she finally handed it to him. It wasn't like she could prevent him from doing it if he really wanted to.

Brant spent a few minutes paging and reading, paging and reading some more. Then he grabbed the phone on the table in front of him and pushed a few buttons. After a few beats, someone on the other end answered.

"Carlyle, would you care to explain a few things to me?" Brant paused while someone talked on the other end. He went on to explain the situation and read out the clauses.

"What do you mean it's a loophole?" he demanded. After a moment, he cursed loudly and more than once. "I know we agreed to tweaking the document, but this is more than a fucking tweak." He listened for half a second. "Don't tell me to calm down."

Brant's eyes were glowing, belying his emotional state. Arousal was obviously not the only catalyst. "You will fix it today and at your own expense or I'm firing your ass. Am I clear?" He listened to the reply. "Good," He snarled, dropping the phone on the table. It was a wonder the screen didn't shatter it fell so hard.

He ran a hand through his hair. Brant pointed at her. "You get to stay on a technicality, under the new terms of payment." He sounded like he was choking on the words. Like it was hurting him to say them.

Cassidy had to force herself to suppress a smile that threatened to crack her face in half.

"The loophole is being rectified as we speak. Everyone will be expected to sign the amendment. If the two of you so much as look at one another again, so help me, there will be hell to pay. Contracts aside, you need to agree to stay away from York for the duration of this trial."

Cassidy nodded grudgingly. "Fine." Even though she and York had agreed that it was only for one night, she still struggled to separate sex from emotions. They'd always gone hand-in-hand before. If she was honest with herself, she liked York and wanted to spend more time with him. She realized it was better if it didn't happen though. It wasn't like they could be together.

"York, I'm not asking you, I'm telling you," Brant narrowed his eyes, "stay away from this female."

Zane made a grunting noise. "I'm curious..." he paused. "Did you drink from the female last night?"

Cassidy could see York hesitate to answer. He glanced at her and then back at the kings. "Two smalls sips." He looked like he wanted to say something else but refrained.

"Twenty lashes, York," Brant said while rising to his feet. "You can't get away with this. An example needs to be made one way or the other."

Cassidy gasped. "What? Lashes? As in across the back? You can't be serious!"

York actually looked relieved, like he had gotten off lightly. He nodded, giving her a reassuring smile. "Twenty lashes is for pussies. It's like a scratch for us vampires. I'll heal in ten minutes. Don't worry about it." He winked at her.

"Careful, I might double it." Brant turned his hard eyes on her. "It will take longer than ten minutes to heal and it will hurt like a bitch."

York growled next to her, she even saw a flash of a fang but he kept his eyes averted.

"There are silver spikes on the end of the whip. As most humans are aware, silver is toxic to us non-humans. His back will be a bleeding mess, the silver will slow the healing process."

Brant was a sick bastard, he actually took pleasure in telling her all this knowing that she would be affected. Cassidy worked hard to keep a handle on her emotions.

Zane turned to Brant. "York doesn't have bloodlust. He said he would prove that he didn't have it and he did."

Something didn't sit right with her about that statement. She wasn't exactly sure what it was. The conversation continued before she could put her finger on it.

"He disobeyed an order. He doesn't deserve a place in the program." Brant raised his brows.

"We said we wanted proven warriors, only the best to continue our line. I hate to tell you but that's him," Zane said as he gestured to where York was standing.

Brant let out a huff of air. "Twenty lashes and you stay away from the humans during the next two days. You can rut all you want when the chosen females arrive. Keep it in your pants until then. For a second there I thought you were turning soft." Brant actually smiled, looking anything but happy. "I thought you really went to see this female to talk with her... to apologize." He was talking about her like she wasn't even in the room. "When your main reason was to prove that you didn't have bloodlust. That's why you rutted her and why you turned yourself in. Fucking genius."

The nagging feeling she couldn't put her finger on. Brant voiced it, summing it up perfectly. Anger and hurt warred inside her. That would explain why such an attractive, out of her league guy was interested in her.

What hurt the most was how he had faked being so

turned on by her. How he genuinely seemed to enjoy her company when it was all an act to ensure that he got enough of her scent on him and vice versa. She felt like a fool for sharing so many private details from her life when in the end, he only wanted to get back in the program. It was all about using her so that he could still get one of the chosen humans so that he could start a family. It was never about her. Never genuine.

"That's not true," York said, but they were just meaningless words. She knew better. People lied and broke trust all the time. Sean had taught her that. It was all about number one in the end, that was what her ex-boss Mark had always maintained. He said it all the time, only she chose not to believe it and she was a fool.

The joke was on her.

Cassidy turned away from York, not wanting to see him. Trying hard not to cry. "If that's all, I'll be leaving now."

Brant didn't move a muscle. "You'll receive your contract amendments before close of business. Be sure to sign them."

She nodded, not trusting her voice.

Brant looked at his watch. "You've missed breakfast, your first session starts in twenty minutes."

Cassidy nodded again while biting onto her lip to try to stop it from quivering. She was such an emotional idiot. It wasn't like she even knew York. There was no way she had any real feelings for him. What was wrong with her? Why the hell was she on the verge of tears? She shouldn't let this get to her.

"Cass…" York said from behind her, his deep voice

washed over her, making her feel so much worse. He had really hurt her. There was no way to stop the feelings of betrayal that coursed through her. At least he wasn't allowed anywhere near her again. She just had to make it out of this room.

Don't cry, Cassidy.

"I'm going now." Her voice came out sounding hard and cold. She didn't even look Brant's way, just turned for the door and began to move.

A warm, calloused hand closed on her wrist. It was a touch she knew all too well. For just a second she allowed his heat to seep into her skin and then she yanked her arm free and fled from the room, sure to slam the door behind her. Cassidy broke into an all-out run, praying that York would not be permitted to follow her. The tears began to flow even before she made it to her suite.

It must have been all the old memories of Sean, of how badly he had hurt her. This whole ordeal had brought things to the surface that were best left buried. She wished she had never met York, that she had never come here in the first place and if she had any other choice she would leave. As it stood, she was sorely tempted to do just that regardless of consequences.

9

ROOM B LOOMED AHEAD.

It was one minute before ten. Cassidy didn't want to linger – she'd timed this perfectly.

Gideon, the vampire head of security, stood to the left of the door. He nodded in greeting and gave her a small smile. His eyes filled with what looked a lot like sympathy mixed with what she could only describe as pity.

Looking away, she held on tighter to her purse strap; she really didn't need this. Not after she'd only just managed to pull herself together. Her eyes were a bit bloodshot and a tad puffy, but mascara and concealer could work wonders. She'd even put a bit of blush and lipstick on to try and appear fresh and upbeat.

"You did good in there earlier," he said as she approached.

When she looked back up, the pity had been replaced with a genuine smile.

"Thanks… I guess."

"No, really." His face turned more serious. "There are very few people who have ever dared to stand up to Brant. Aside from his mate and one other female, you are the only human who's ever done it. You deserve to still be here." He looked around them, speaking softly. "York pulled a serious dick move. I've never known him to act in such a way. I know that he really wants a family. I just can't believe he would treat you so badly in order to reach that end. It's not on you though and I want you to know that. I plan on having a talk with him about it." He took a step closer to her, again looking around to make sure that no one was listening in. "I know how emotional human females are when it comes to sex. The only consolation I can give you is that he doesn't realize how bad this has made you feel, and if he does, he doesn't fully understand why. I don't believe he intended to hurt you."

"I'm not hurt," she blurted. "I hardly know him." She tried to play it down.

"I could scent how hurt you were. I can still scent it on you even though it is underlying."

Fuckity fuck.

That meant that they all had smelled it on her. She'd prayed that she had looked and seemed more together than she actually was, not thinking for a minute that her blasted scent had given her away. *Vampires sucked!*

"I felt used. Like an idiot. I'm fine now. Thanks, I appreciate it." Maybe they weren't all so bad.

Gideon nodded. "I will keep a close eye on you. Just shout if you need anything. Do you still remember the safe word?"

Cassidy nodded. "As if I could forget." Just thinking of it made her heart squeeze and her eyes tear. It made her think of last night, reminded her of York. *The big, fat jerk.* If she ever saw his face again it would be too soon. "Can we maybe use another word?"

Gideon looked confused for a second, and then he shrugged. "Sure, what did you have in mind?"

"Um… 'noodles,' maybe?" *Pumpkin.* She'd never been overly fond of vegetables.

Gideon broke into a smile. He nodded once. "Noodles it is then. I'll just brief the guards as well as the ladies in the comms room and we're all set."

"Thanks again." She did feel a little bit better.

"Anytime." Gideon pulled out a two-way radio. "Be safe in there and don't forget the new safe word."

"I won't," she said as she continued towards the door.

"Comms room B, Comms room B come in…" There was a clicking noise and the sound of static before a woman's voice crackled over the system.

Cassidy couldn't make out what she was saying because she entered the room and closed the door behind her.

The vampire was sitting sprawled out on the sofa. Although very tall, he wasn't nearly as built as York.

Stop it.

She had to try and get that asshole right out of her head.

He moved swiftly to his feet, rubbing his hands on his jeans. By now she was getting used to how attractive vampires were and wasn't affected at all by his wide, dimpled grin. He looked a bit younger than the others she had met. There was an air of mischief about him. "Hi, I'm Griffin." He extended a hand, which she took.

Not nearly as big or as warm as…

Stop it.

"It's really nice to meet you, Griffin." She found herself smiling despite the nervous tension.

He raised his brow, his lips still turned up at the edges. "You have amazing eyes… though I'm sure you've been told that dozens of times."

"Thank you." Although she had received a ton of compliments over the years, she hadn't had many recently. These vampires were all a bunch of charmers, that was for sure.

"You don't have to be nervous."

"That's what the big, bad wolf said to Little Red Riding Hood and he tried to eat her," she muttered.

Griffin chuckled. "I don't know much about girls wearing red hoods and I'm not a wolf shifter." His voice was a low growl. Not nearly as deep and gruff sounding as…

Stop it!

Dammit, she was getting irritated with herself.

Griffin winked at her. "I'm a vampire, which means that if I wanted to eat you I wouldn't have to try, I would just go ahead and do it." His nostrils flared and she realized that he could smell what had gone down last night.

It made her blood heat and not in the way he was hoping. Cassidy put her hands on her hips. "Like hell you would. You probably think I'm some easy, idiot human. Well, I've got news for you, if you think that I'm letting you or any of your kind anywhere near me again, you're deluding yourself."

Griffin's eyes widened and his brow creased. He put up his hands. "I didn't mean anything by it. I'm sorry if I offended you." He looked genuinely sorry. Even had the whole 'puppy dog' look down pat.

"It's fine, it's just I'm not used to everyone knowing my very private business. I don't like it," she mumbled the last.

"Just so you know, vampires see rutting as just one of those things. We view it as something that needs to happen, like breathing or eating. It's not a big deal. I thought you would've received this information in your training." He hooked his thumbs into his jeans.

"Not really, since we weren't actually allowed to have sex."

Griffin chuckled. "York has big balls to have touched you. He will be sorry later when he goes under the whip. I've only ever had ten lashes and that was bad enough."

Don't feel sorry for him Cassidy. Don't you dare feel sorry. He used you.

"I can't believe you're not up for a round two though." Griffin lifted his brows, that mischievous glint was back. "He can't have done it right if you don't want more." It was delivered so innocently that she had to laugh. "Not that I'm suggesting anything," he quickly added, a big grin on his face. "I swear."

Despite his words, she did notice that his eyes dipped to her breasts before returning to her face...

make that her mouth. He was checking her out. God, these vampires were certainly an oversexed bunch. "Um…" He lifted his eyes to meet hers. "Do you want me to touch you while I…" He rubbed a hand through his hair.

Motherfucker!

York was going to punch the shit out of Griffin directly after this session was over. If he so much as laid a finger on her, he wasn't sure he could wait until the session was over. His hands clenched at his sides and he suppressed a growl.

"What are you doing in here?" Sasha asked as she swiveled in her chair to face him. "This is a restricted area."

Lea glanced at him over her shoulder, a small smile toyed with the corners of her full lips. "Hey, York. I haven't seen you much lately." Loosely translated, he hadn't rutted with her in a while.

He smiled back. "Hi, Lea."

Her smile grew. "I can scent that you have been playing with the humans. You naughty thing you." She licked her lips. "I hear you are getting twenty lashes for it as well." She pulled a face for a few seconds before smiling again. "You should come to me later… I'll fix you right up."

"Yeah, sounds like a plan." Normally he would've jumped at the opportunity. Lea was attractive and they were highly compatible. The thought didn't appeal to him at the moment as much as it should have though.

"You can leave now." Sasha turned her hard eyes on him.

"Please, let me stay," York tried not to sound desperate.

"Males are not permitted to watch. Humans become embarrassed when our males ease them."

The thought of Griffin's hands on Cassidy infuriated him. Schooling his expression and working hard to get a handle on his emotions, York nodded. "This female will not let Griffin touch her."

Lea laughed. Even Sasha cracked a smile. "They all let the males touch them. Every single human, every single time without fail," Lea said.

"It's true," Sasha added. "The agreement is that we can monitor them, so long as it is a female who does the monitoring. That means that you have to leave… now." Her voice held a hard edge.

"I will leave if she allows him to touch her." He could barely get the words around the lump in his throat. "I am merely concerned for her safety. Griffin is still young." *That was it… yes…* Her safety was at the forefront of his mind.

Lea gave a quick laugh. "That's the human you rutted? Am I right? Please don't tell me you have feelings for her."

York scowled. "No way. I guess I feel I owe her. I don't want to see her hurt. That is all." The female was really sweet. Brant had gone and fucked everything up. Cassidy had been badly hurt. He owed her this much.

"There are three guards outside that room. You really don't need to be here." Lea glanced at him before returning her gaze to the screen.

York shrugged. "Humor me... please."

Sasha grinned. "I guess it's nothing you haven't seen before anyway." She too put her focus back on the screen.

"Keep quiet and no one finds out about this or we will all be in serious trouble." Lea didn't look comfortable.

Tough luck, he was staying. York felt his blood boil as Griffin alluded to eating Cassidy. Little dickhead was going to cry like a baby by the time he was done with him. He almost laughed out loud and fist punched the air when Cassidy put him in his place, even though her words didn't sit right with him.

She'd said that she wasn't going to let him or any other vampire near her again. The pain in her voice and her eyes was evident. He wished he could see her and explain things but that's what had caused all this shit last time. He was back in the program and forbidden to see Cassidy. It would be better if she finished up here and moved on with her life.

In order for that to happen, he would make sure that she got through the next six sessions alive and well. York didn't care who he needed to bribe or beg to make that happen, only that it would. He wasn't technically in breach of his agreement with Brant since he wasn't in the same room as her.

He narrowed his eyes at the screen. The little prick was mentally undressing Cassidy. Griffin's eyes were glued to her breasts. By the way Cassidy squirmed, he could see that she was uncomfortable under the scrutiny.

Um…" Griffin lifted his eyes to meet hers. "Do you want me to touch you while I…" He ran a hand through his hair.

Little shit didn't just say that?

York knew he was being irrational, it was the exact same question he had asked the previous day. Problem was, he couldn't seem to help himself.

"No… thank you," Cassidy quickly answered and he was able to take a breath into his starving lungs. *Thank the gods.*

Griffin's beady little eyes lowered back to her chest for half a beat. "Are you sure? It might get a little difficult for you. I wouldn't mind at all."

I'm sure you fucking wouldn't!

Cassidy threw Griffin a small smile that looked sad. York felt it inside himself. A funny feeling in his chest. It didn't feel good. He really liked Cassidy, she was a good person who had been hurt before. York hated that he had been the one to hurt her this time around. *Fucking hated it!*

"No, I'm good thanks. I assure you that I won't need you to —" she paused, "to touch me in any way."

Griffin shrugged. "Suit yourself. Let me know if you change your mind."

She won't.

Lea turned her head slightly, still keeping her eyes on the screen in front of her. "Shhhh."

York realized that he had spoken out loud and pressed his lips together to prevent any further outbursts. He also shoved his hands in his pockets.

Griffin removed his shirt and sat back down on the sofa. "Get more comfortable and take a seat." He gestured to his lap.

Cassidy removed her jacket, turning and folding it neatly before bending to place it on top of her purse.

There were several cameras in the room, placed in various positions. York ground his teeth together watching how Griffin checked out Cassidy's ass as she bent down. The male even repositioned his dick in his pants. The fucker was hard for her. York had to close his eyes for a few seconds to keep himself under control.

"You might want to lose the dress."

York shook his head, running a hand over the buzz on his scalp. The neckline on Cassidy's dress was a little lower than the blouse had been yesterday. Not low enough to reveal even a hint of cleavage but low enough that her neck was sufficiently exposed. The little prick was trying his luck, plain and simple.

Cassidy shook her head, giving Griffin a hint of a smile. "I think you'll manage."

Thank the gods up above, she sat down next to Griffin instead of sitting on his lap and turned her head away from him. Her legs were crossed at the knee and her hands were clasped in her lap. There was no sign of the sensual female he had caught a glimpse of the night before.

It should've helped to make him feel a bit better about this whole thing. Should've had his heart slowing down, should've stopped the adrenaline that surged through his veins. It didn't. He still felt like he was slowly suffocating. Like a great weight was coming down on him.

York didn't want Griffin to touch her. Not a hair on

her head. Not so much as a chaste touch with the tip of a single finger. He most definitely did not want the male drinking from her.

"Ready?" Griffin asked.

Cassidy nodded.

When Griffin leaned forward and buried his head in her neck, York not only growled but he snarled as well causing both Lea and Sasha to gasp.

Cassidy's eyes widened for a quick second before clamping shut. Another even louder snarl was torn from him as he watched Griffin's throat work as he swallowed the first mouthful of her blood.

York didn't think. If he had allowed rational thought to enter his mind, he would've stayed right where he was and dealt with his feelings; instead he acted. Within seconds he had busted the door to room B clear off its hinges and ripped Griffin from Cassidy.

That was not where it ended, he punched the male in the face three times. The first one pulverized his nose, the second cracked his jaw and the last split both his top and bottom lips in a spray of blood. York moved into position to kick Griffin in the ribs, trying to aim correctly for most impact. A broken sternum was one of the most difficult bones in the body to heal. It hurt like hell. Unfortunately, the guards outside chose just that moment to rain on his parade and pulled him back.

Three of the fuckers.

York still managed to land a few punches while they worked to secure him. Griffin was dazed and bleeding. Red and wet looked good on the fucker. He only wished he'd had a bit more time to make him pay for touching his female. *The female.* He had no hold over Cassidy. He didn't even know her.

When he turned to her, she was pale. "What's wrong with you?" She looked away as she reached for her bag.

"Let me explain—" York began.

"I think you've done enough explaining. Please leave me alone. You're ruining my life." She put the purse strap around her shoulder and practically ran out of the room.

The ache in his chest was back. He didn't know how to get rid of it. Hitting Griffin had only made him feel worse. York put a hand to his chest, the distraught look on Cassidy's face had physically hurt him. He didn't know how to fix this.

10

"**I** CANNOT BELIEVE THAT you went against my orders within an hour of my giving them!" Brant smashed his fist into the table. It cracked, right down the middle. He cursed. "Look what you made me do."

He pushed a couple of buttons on his phone and held the device to his ear. "Allison..." It was Brant's personal assistant. "Please order another boardroom table."

There was a chuckle on the other end. Allison said something in reply. York was too deep in his own thoughts to pay much attention.

"Yes," Brant barked, "another one."

"This will be the second one you've ruined this month," Brant's assistant said.

"Get me a stronger table then." He ended the call.

His king sucked in a deep breath. "What the fuck am I going to do with you?" He rose to his feet and moved to the other end of the room, running a hand through his hair. "There is a reason why you head up the elite team, York." He paused for a few beats. "Yeah sure, you're strong. One of the most capable warriors in battle, but you are more than just those things." He turned to face York, his eyes were blazing. "You are responsible, you keep your cool in the most difficult situations. I need a level-headed leader and I thought I had one in you."

Brant didn't say anything for the longest time. York had to work to keep from fidgeting.

"Where has my sensible leader gone? I don't even fucking know you. Sneaking around to get into some human female's pants. Breaking rules. Not to mention that you fucked Griffin up royally. Might have even killed him if the guards hadn't pulled you off – and for no reason other than that he was touching that human. Do you know how this looks?"

His king didn't wait for a reply. "Bad, York. Fucking bad. I should demote you and kick you out of this program, but I'm going to give you one last chance. I must be mad," he mumbled.

York wanted to thank his king. Brant was not one for granting favors... ever. He couldn't though, the words stuck in his throat.

"I'm sending the human away."

"No," York growled, earning himself a hard slap. He didn't flinch, didn't move a muscle. He welcomed the sting. The taste of his blood from his inner cheek as it was crushed against his teeth by the force of the blow.

"Yes," Brant growled back just as harshly. "She is making you crazy for some reason. She goes – today – right now and as we speak. I will pay her out in full since this isn't her fault."

"Thank you." He meant it. At least Cassidy wouldn't be punished for his mistake.

"This is for the best. Trust me. Once she's gone you can go back to being my dependable leader again." He walked the length of the room before turning back to York. "Stay away from her. The humans intended as future mates will be here within a few days. I am sure that there will be one amongst them that draws your attention." Brant smiled. "It was your first taste of a human. They are sweet and will fire a vampire's blood. I don't really blame you for getting carried away, but it stops now."

Brant was probably right. Although he hated the thought of Cassidy leaving, it was for the best.

"One of the other females will be just as delicious, you will see," Brant smiled.

What his king said made sense.

York nodded and took a deep breath. "I am ready for my punishment."

Brant raised a brow. "You will still get twenty lashes."

York felt his brow furrow. Brant's eyes darkened. *Here it comes. There has to be more.* His king would never let such a blatant disregard of orders go unpunished. "Sasha and Lea will join you. I've decided to go easy on them – five lashes each."

York couldn't help the low growl that erupted. It was very rare that a vampire female was ever punished in such a way. "No," York snapped. "It's my fault. I talked them into letting me watch."

"They broke the rules and need to make amends."

"There has to be another way, my lord. Five lashes… it's too much." York implored his king with his eyes. Surely Brant would not be that cruel.

"It should be more than five. I am going easy on them and you know it."

Like hell.

"They are going to be pissed off with you. That's for sure." There was no humor in Brant's expression, or in his voice for that matter.

"No. It is too much for a female. It's not right," York insisted. "I will take their punishment for them."

"Thirty lashes will put you down for a while." Brant's eyes darkened.

"I don't care. It is my fault so I will accept the punishment. I insist."

Brant kept his eyes on York, his expression was unreadable. "Fine." He finally shrugged. "Whatever makes you feel better. This is that last time I let you off easy."

Easy?

Hardly! Thirty lashes would leave his back a raw, bloody mess. There was one thought that would get him through the next few hours of excruciating pain though: he had hurt Cassidy. He hadn't meant to do it, but he had. York couldn't help but feel that he deserved everything he had coming.

A loud crack sounded. It caused her to start, it had her breath seizing in her lungs.

"Please don't tell me…" she let the sentence die as her voice hitched. York may be a jerk but he didn't deserve such harsh treatment. It was downright barbaric.

Gideon sighed loudly. He moved Cassidy's bag from one hand to the other. "Yeah, I'm afraid that it's exactly what it sounds like."

Yet another sharp crack. Louder this time.

Cassidy held her breath. The harsh noise was followed by eerie silence.

"Thirty lashes," Gideon sighed again. "York will take a day or two to recover."

Crack.

"I thought he was only getting twenty," Cassidy blurted.

"Only…?" Gideon raised his brows. He choked out something that resembled a laugh.

"I didn't mean it like that." Cassidy turned her eyes to the ground.

Crack. She swallowed hard, hugging herself with her arms. She'd never heard anything like it before, was sure that the noise would haunt her dreams… her nightmares.

Gideon nodded. "I know you didn't and I'm sorry. It's a harsh punishment and all of us are on edge right now."

Crack.

The big vampire visibly started, it was strange to see such a strong man affected like that.

"Why doesn't he react? He should scream or groan or something. Surely?" Her voice was a little shrill. She noticed that they had both picked up the pace. She couldn't stand to hear it any more. The noise seemed to reverberate through her bones.

"York is a great warrior. The best we have. The elite pride themselves on their control… at all times. By doing what he did with you, he showed a total lack of control. It is his way of making amends. Besides, only pussies show pain. York is no pussy!" He growled the last.

Crack.

Cassidy sucked in a deep breath, holding it inside herself for a few beats. Vampires were harsh, primal creatures. It was one of the things that had attracted her to York in the first place. Right now, she hated that side of them though. Needed to get as far away as possible.

"Please do not try and contact York again." There was a hard edge to Gideon's voice. "A relationship between the two of you is forbidden. Any type of contact would only end in heartbreak." He swallowed hard, his throat working overtime. For a second, a look of sadness crossed his face. It was gone almost as soon as it had arrived. "That type of suffering is not worth it in the long run. Please take my word for it. The two of you have not spent much time together, it is still possible to go your separate ways."

She wasn't really sure what he was talking about. Gideon spoke as if there was genuinely something between her and York, which was not true. He had used her plain and simple. Unfortunately, she was wired to feel something for someone she had slept with so she did harbor feelings for him but after just one night together, those feelings were nothing. Less than nothing.

Crack.

Cassidy squeezed her eyes shut, trying not to picture York's bloody back, his anguished face – and failed dismally. "You have it all wrong," she finally said. "It was just sex." She shrugged. "I was curious and he had something to prove... simple."

Gideon nodded, his eyes held a glint of... humor. Like he didn't buy it. Well, let him think what he wanted, she knew better. There was no rational explanation for York tearing into Griffin like that, but she was not going to fool herself into thinking it had anything to do with her.

Crack.

Vampires were no better than animals. They probably went at each other all the time.

They made it to her beat-up little car and she found herself praying it would start. The good news was that she had money. Lots of it. True to his word, Brant had deposited the agreed-upon sum into her account.

Cassidy should be happy. She'd essentially earned money for doing nothing. Instead, her heart felt heavy. Her mind worked overtime, dissecting all the events of the last two days.

Crack.

"Thank you for everything." She said, trying to move as quickly as possible.

Gideon deposited her bag in the trunk. "Please take my advice."

Cassidy nodded. "You have nothing to worry about."

Gideon closed the trunk "I'm not worried for myself... nothing good will come of it. Trust me, I know." He sounded like he spoke from experience. A look of hurt crossed his face again.

"I'm leaving, not only here but Sweetwater. I'll be gone within a day or two. York and I don't have each other's contact info. I told you it wasn't like that... at least not for him." She sucked in a breath. What had she just said? "Or for me," she quickly added. "It wasn't like that."

Crack.

The sound ripped through her and tears welled in her eyes. Why was she feeling like this? Over a guy who had used her... hurt her.

Crack.

The falls of the whip were coming faster now. Her tears threatened to overflow and her lip quivered so she bit down on it. "I really have to go now," she whispered while getting into the car and rolling down her window.

Gideon nodded. "Good luck. Don't worry about him, he will be fine."

Crack.

Her whole body jumped and she put a hand to her heart, quickly starting up her engine. It clanked and rattled but it turned over and continued to run even when she revved it a few times.

They said a quick goodbye and she pulled away slowly.

Crack.

A loud anguished growl had her standing on the brakes. She looked in the rearview mirror. Gideon looked shocked, his head was turned slightly in the direction of the sound. To where York was being beaten. A tear fell but she wiped it away, pushing down on her accelerator. The engine roared and clanked back to life as she continued to move.

Crack.

A tormented wail tore through her, making her whimper. The tears flowed freely and she struggled to see the road ahead but she kept her foot pressed down. Kept on moving away.

11

One week later . . .

YORK PULLED UP TO the club. Although humans were
not permitted in Aorta, a long, thick queue of them
wrapped halfway around the block. Most of those
trying to get in were females. When Brant's club had
first opened a year or two ago, humans had tried to get
in constantly but after a few months of failing, the
attempts mostly dried up. It was only when word got
out that one of the kings was in attendance that things
became a little chaotic. Thankfully that wasn't very
often anymore. Not since they had mated Tanya, and
not at all since the royal heir had been born. York had
to smile just thinking of the little tyke. Those chubby
little hands and cheeks were the cutest things ever. His
favorite was when little Sam was tired. His big,
gummy yawns made him feel all warm inside.

A group of females surged forward as they caught
sight of his SUV, pulling him out of his thoughts.

Word was out about the breeding program and the opportunities it afforded human females when it came to mating with vampire males and *boom,* things were back to being an utter mess outside Aorta.

He was glad that he didn't have to control the chaos. Gideon would have his hands full. The male could be seen talking and listening on an earpiece. There was a whole bevy of guards outside the club and he knew there would be many more inside.

This was the first time the ten elite were meeting with the chosen human females. York glanced at his watch, already knowing what he would see. He was late by about half an hour. *Tough luck.* At least he was here. His mind wandered to little Sam and his own drive to have a family. It was something he felt on an instinctual level. The need to procreate.

Yet, after dreaming of this moment for months, he felt completely deflated. There were human females inside. Ones he was actually permitted to touch, yet the thought left him cold.

You haven't even seen them yet.

Maybe one of them would spark the same interest he had for Cassidy. *Don't dwell on recent events. Move forward.*

Taking in a deep breath, he pulled his SUV into one of the reserved parking spots. Three guards approached the vehicle, holding a group of human females at bay. The humans were of varying ages, from 'barely legal' to 'needing a walker.' Didn't they have anything better to do?

"About damned time," Gideon muttered as he exited the vehicle.

For a second, York thought to apologize but in the end he let it slide. "Have all the best females been taken?" He'd hoped to sound light-hearted but failed dismally.

Gideon smiled. "Glad to see that you are doing better. How's the back?"

York shrugged. "No big deal. It healed quickly enough." He hadn't seen the male since that day in the boardroom.

Gideon chuckled. "By the way you howled like a baby, I would've thought you'd be down a lot longer."

Clenching his teeth, he didn't answer for a few beats. The males had given him huge slack for not remaining silent during his beating. Hearing Cassidy start her car, hearing her leave. It had cut him deeper than any silver spike ever could. He didn't understand it. Lust could turn even the hardest male into a blithering idiot but that wasn't it. Maybe it was because it killed him that she thought the worst of him. That she felt he was ruining her life. Cassidy thought that he had used her to get back into the program. He wished he could go and see her to explain – just one damn time – but she was right, so far his meddling had caused shit for her. For them both. He really was a masochist because he'd lifted her file, had looked up her address even though he never planned on ever actually using the information. Regardless of how much he wanted to.

Gideon must have seen something written on his face because he tapped him on the shoulder. "I'm only joking around. I know your whining had nothing to do with receiving those lashes."

York scowled at the male. He didn't particularly feel like discussing it with him. They both moved to the front entrance of the club. The guards did a good job of keeping the females away.

"I was with the human when she left. It wasn't lost on me how you didn't make another sound after she was gone." Gideon shook his head. "The humans inside are stunning," he pointed to the club, "or so I have heard. You need to give it a chance. Maybe you will meet the right one."

"You haven't seen them yet?" York raised a brow.

Gideon shook his head. "It's been hectic out here since early evening. Somehow information about tonight must have leaked despite the heavy confidentiality clauses. I have my hands full." He shrugged. "Besides, it's not like any of them are here for me, so what's the point?"

They arrived at the large double doors of the club. "Why didn't you try out for the program?" York asked. "You could easily have made the top ten."

Gideon shrugged again, looking distinctly uncomfortable. "I'm not the settling down type. I don't particularly want a mate, or children for that matter." His eyes darkened.

It didn't make sense to York. Most males he knew would give their right testicle to be included. "I can't say I understand, but whatever makes you happy."

Gideon glanced at the growing crowd. "I need to get back to work." He clenched his teeth. "If this gets any worse I'm going to have to call for backup. The kings insisted that this whole thing take place at Aorta. They felt the human females would feel more comfortable in a relaxed setting. Fucking crazy if you ask me."

York nodded. "Especially with the recent attempt on Zane's life." His chopper had been shot down by a group of fascist humans with a vendetta against the vampires. Particularly the kings. The group was not thrilled at the prospect of human women being taken as mates by vampire males. They had managed to capture one of the members who had shot Zane but in a fit of rage, Brant had killed the male before he could give up much information. It left them in the dark as to how many of them there were. How organized and skilled they were. More importantly, as to who they were and what their futures plans were.

The threat could be nothing… and it could be very real. They were treating it as the latter.

York nodded. "Thanks for seeing Cassidy off the other day, and for the advice."

"For the record, I know you didn't use her like Brant thinks you did. You need to know that it doesn't help to go against the system. Our rules are in place for a reason." He sighed heavily. "We may not like them, but we have to obey them." Gideon smiled. "Now, go inside and find your future mate."

York nodded back. "I'll see you later."

"Sure thing." Gideon turned and walked away, he already had a phone to his ear within two strides. All business.

York turned back to the entrance. The guards at the door greeted him with big smiles.

"You are so damn lucky," one said as he walked past.

"They are just as sweet as we have been told," another remarked.

He ignored the male. Ignored them all as he walked inside.

An upbeat song played. The club was not very big as it was specially designed for vampire patrons only. The interior was distinctly modern and highly tasteful. It was Brant's club, and that meant that no expense had been spared. Marble, crystal and silver were the main finishes. Light, clean and elegant with a minimalistic flair. He'd always enjoyed coming here. He'd always picked up a vampire female on the few times he'd been here during leisure time. Would he get so lucky tonight? Did he even want to? Thing was, he really needed to move on. Once and for all. One night with Cassidy was hardly a relationship. They had both been clear that it was a one-time thing.

Fuck!

Why was he even thinking about her again? She had probably already left town like she said she wanted to. York was sure that she had moved on without another thought. No more dwelling on what could never be.

There were a lot of females in attendance. Delicious scents tantalized his senses. A quick count brought the total number of females in sight, to twenty-two. Ten males and at least twenty-two females. Brant was obviously useless at math.

Griffin had his arm around one of the females. She pressed her body against him and whispered something in his ear. Some of the guys were talking with more than one female. Lance had three females surrounding him. A pretty boy player regardless of whether the female was human or vampire. It seemed that his whole brooding, intense thing worked on all females. It turned out that despite his foul temper, Lance didn't have bloodlust. Only one of the males was afflicted. A quiet, reserved male. *Go fucking figure.*

"About damned time." Lazarus appeared from nowhere. His friend wore a tank top exposing thick, well-muscled arms that would surely scare away the timid humans.

"It doesn't look like I've missed much." York folded his arms across his chest.

Lazarus made a groaning noise. "Just heaven… they are so damned pretty."

"So why are you here talking to me instead of them?"

Lazarus took on a pained expression. "I'm not much of a talker." The male was right, he grunted more than he spoke.

"I tried to start up a conversation with that little blonde over there." He pointed to the bar. A woman in high heels and a seriously tight dress was ordering a drink. "I introduced myself and then panicked." Lazarus' eyes dropped and he sucked in a deep breath.

"What did you do?"

He looked down at his feet. "I told her she had stunning mammary glands."

York had to laugh. "We were taught to go easy on the compliments. You should've talked about her eyes or her hair."

"Yeah, but look at her." Lazarus moaned as the female turned around and sure enough, there was enough cleavage in her low-cut dress to sink whole ships. Big cruise liners for that matter. "I suck at this. You should've seen her face. I'm surprised she didn't slap me."

York chuckled. "Relax. We have plenty of such meet and greet sessions planned over the next few weeks. There are more humans than males, I'm sure one of them will be interested in a testosterone-riddled, huge motherfucker like you."

Lazarus flexed his muscles. "Better believe it," he responded.

"About that though..." York made for the bar and Lazarus stayed next to him. "You should look for a shirt like mine." York ran his hands down the dress shirt he was wearing. "You could also use a pair of jeans." He glanced at the other male's leather pants. York choked out a laugh. "And for fuck's sakes lose the knives."

Lazarus had a blade strapped at his thigh and another on his belt. He knew that there would be more concealed weapons on him. The other male scowled. "What if we are attacked?" His jaw ticked. "I need to be ready to protect the humans. They are weak and easily hurt."

"They are also easily scared." York ordered a drink for himself. He decided on a beer. It was a perfectly acceptable human drink. He noticed that many of the males had one in their hands. "Do you want anything?"

"Blood... hold the ice," Lazarus requested.

York raised a brow at the male.

"What?" Lazarus put up his hands. "Okay fine," he exhaled, "blood and a double shot of vodka."

"You can't drink blood in front of the humans." York kept his voice low. "Were you not paying any attention in the training sessions?"

"I'm a fucking vampire," Lazarus growled so loudly that he made one of the females to the right of them shriek and grab her chest. "Sorry," he mumbled while taking a step towards her.

She visibly paled. The female swallowed hard and nodded. "It's f-fine," she stammered, her eyes wide.

As soon as Lazarus turned back towards him, the female slunk away, glancing back in their direction every so often. Human females were terrified of him. Then again, full grown vampire males were terrified of Lazarus so he didn't blame them.

"I understand that you are a vampire but you can tone it down while they are getting to know you. This is new to them."

"Screw that. I am who I am," he answered, in true Lazarus style.

"Don't listen to me then. You can order your own damn blood," York said, keeping his voice down. He noticed that there was a female sitting at the end of the bar. She looked lost, her eyes kept moving around the room. It was like she was searching for something... or someone. "Take those blades off and hand them in at the bar. Let's go and speak to that female over there." He pointed her out to Lazarus without making it obvious.

"Yeah," Lazarus rumbled. "She has stunning eyes. So very big..." He bobbed his eyebrows up and down. "And her hair is fucking lush and curvy... I mean wavy." He bobbed his brows a second time. York had to laugh. He noted that the male removed the visible knives, but he didn't end up ordering anything to drink.

They made their way over to the female. York held his beer, taking a sip every so often. It tasted pretty shitty and the alcohol content was too low to even give him a mild buzz. If it made the humans feel more comfortable though, then he didn't mind drinking it.

The female seemed taken aback that they had approached her. She didn't look particularly happy by the way she pressed her lips together and she pulled her purse more tightly against her midsection. Her heart-rate picked up.

"Would you mind if we joined you?" he asked. "You look a little lonely sitting all the way over here on your own."

"I'm fine over here on my own..." Her eyes widened. "But I wouldn't mind *talking* for a while." She emphasized the word 'talking.' Contrary to how quickly he and Cassidy had ended up in bed together, human women tended to prefer a drawn-out courtship. He didn't understand it. This must be one of those females.

"I'm York and this is Lazarus."

"I'm Jenna." She shook both their hands in turn. The good news was that she didn't seem too afraid of Lazarus. She even gave him a shy smile. "Is everyone here?" she asked, still craning her neck to take a good look around the room.

"I'm not sure," York answered. "I think all the females are here. How many of you made it through? I was only expecting for there to be ten. Since there are ten of us."

Jenna finally turned her gaze back to him and Lazarus. "Um… there are twenty-five of us. We were warned that not all of us would be chosen." Then her eyes swept back across the space. "I was talking about vampires. Are all of you here tonight?"

Lazarus gave a grunt of affirmation.

The female even lifted slightly off her chair to get a better view of the club.

"Are you looking for someone?" York had to ask. It was glaringly obvious that she was.

Her face turned bright red and she vehemently shook her head. "No… I mean yes… one of the other girls. I said I would keep an eye out for her. She must be in the ladies room or something."

"All of the males are here." York said, watching her face cloud in disappointment.

What the hell?

"Hi there." A really pretty female came up and joined their small group. She moved in right next to York, turning her eyes on him. "I'm Vanessa."

"There you are." The shy female smiled broadly. "This is York and that's Lazarus." Jenna gestured to each of them. Maybe she had been waiting on her friend after all.

Vanessa had long blond hair and just about the bluest eyes York had ever seen. Like all the humans who had been chosen for them, she was both tiny – in a way that only a human could be – and curvaceous – also in a way that only a human could be. Her hips were wide, made for holding onto. Her ass was so lush, it should've had his hands itching for a grab.

Her breasts were like two pillows. The perfect cradle for both his mouth and head. His dick should be jumping out of his pants by now, yet... nothing. Not even a twitch.

The female visibly flinched when she shook Lazarus' big hand and even took a step closer to York. She scented of cinnamon bathed in vanilla. His mouth didn't so much as water and his fangs stayed firmly in his gums.

Fuck!

York took a quick look around the club, really looking at the human females for the first time. When it came to looks and scent, Vanessa was right up there. One of the sexiest humans in the room. Lance glared daggers at him. Two guesses on who the male had picked as a possible prospect. It almost made York want to put his arm around the female.

If only he was in the least bit interested.

"So..." Vanessa pulled her full lower lip into her mouth for a few beats. "I'm seriously hoping that since you are here, that you are one of the eligible vampire bachelors."

York nodded. "Yeah, I am." Maybe if he chatted with her for a bit. "What made you decide to be a part of all of this?"

"What? Are you kidding? You guys are so incredible! You live in a castle... you're seriously wealthy. What girl in her right mind wouldn't jump at the chance? By the look of the mass of women," she giggled, "and even a couple of men out there, I'd say that loads would agree with me." She smiled, looking up at him through her lashes.

"Reality can sometimes be very different from fantasy."

"Honey…" Her eyes moved over him in a way that should've had something firing up inside him. "I'm looking at the reality and you're even better than any fantasy I have ever had. May I?" She put a manicured hand out, wanting to touch him.

York grit his teeth. Surely her hands on him mingled with her exotic scent would rouse him from whatever it was that was wrong with him? He nodded.

The scent of her arousal kicked up a notch as her hand smoothed over his chest, her fingers brushed lightly over his pecs before crossing to his biceps where she gave a squeeze. "Wow!" She breathed the word rather than said it. "You sure are stacked. Makes me want to know if you're like that everywhere." She kept her hand where it was for a few beats, her eyes stayed locked with his.

For blood's sake! The female didn't waste any time. The last thing he wanted was for her to think that he was interested because he really wasn't. Not even a little.

"I've decided to take my time getting to know all of the human females. I don't want to rush into anything and neither should you." He sounded like a total pussy. It almost felt like the roles had been reversed.

Vanessa licked her lips. Her tongue slowly dragged over them in a sensual, well-practiced move that did nothing for him. Normally this type of display by a really hot female would lead to equally hot sex. The problem was that he wasn't here for a fuck, he was here to find a mate. Sure, compatibility would have to be tested but there needed to be more there to begin with. York suppressed a yawn.

Vanessa must have sensed that she was losing him because she pressed herself against him. Her lush curves should have felt really good but all he could think about was Cassidy. Her unique green-tinged eyes, her honeyed skin, the splash of freckles across her nose. She had no idea how utterly intoxicating she was. How sensual and sweet. It was a combination that had brought him to his knees then and made him want to find her now.

Vanessa cleared her throat in an effort to draw his attention. "That's exactly what I'm suggesting… that we get to know each other a bit better. We were briefed on how sexual vampires are. You don't have to hold back on my account." Her eyes traveled the length of him. "I'm game if you are."

"We are not permitted to fuck tonight and I'm a stickler for rules," York said, trying not to growl at her.

Lazarus barked out a laugh that sounded raw and gravelly. York threw his friend a dirty look, hoping he would shut the hell up.

Vanessa shrugged, her fingers played on her skin in the vicinity of her cleavage. It was an invitation to look. York declined by keeping his eyes on hers.

"There are plenty of other things we could do. Besides, we're allowed to have at each other from tomorrow on. Tonight could be a practice run." She was clearly used to getting her way.

"Thank you, but I would rather we…" Damn but he had turned into a serious pussy. "Talk."

This resulted in another laugh from Lazarus. He

and the shy female were, at least, making small talk.

The female in front of him looked crestfallen for a second before her eyes hardened up. "Suit yourself. I can see that you're not interested." She turned and headed back to Lance, draping herself over him. Much to the dismay of a sweet looking female who had been talking with him. The idiot male put his arms around Vanessa, he even cupped her ass with both his hands.

York felt nothing but relief.

As much as he wanted a female and a family, he couldn't move on without properly explaining things to Cassidy. It ate at him that she thought badly of him. That she thought he had used her. The worst part of it was that it would affect her self-confidence and her ability to trust again. The thought of her with another male angered the hell out of him but the thought of her all alone made him feel even worse. He had to set the record straight. Then he would actually be able to give one of these females the time of day.

Unfortunately, Gideon would know exactly what he was up to if he tried to leave early.

"What made you join the program?" Lazarus asked.

"I'm looking for a vampire," Jenna answered.

Lazarus gave a rough bark of a laugh. "You came to the right place."

"I sure hope so," the female answered. She didn't seem afraid of Lazarus but she also didn't seem interested in him. In fact, she didn't seem in the least bit interested in any of the males.

"Can I get either of you a drink?" York interjected. If he was going to have to hang around, he would try to make the most of it.

There was screaming from outside. Loud, hysterical screaming. Guards streamed into the club, at least ten of them. They positioned themselves at various points within the club interior. York noted that the entrances were all covered.

Jenna pulled her bag closer to her chest. Her eyes became saucers in her skull and her heart-rate kicked into overdrive. York could scent her fear.

"What the fuck's going on?" Lazarus snarled at one of the leather clad guards. The male looked alert and ready.

"Someone threw a pig carcass onto the pavement in front of Aorta followed by a bucket of blood. The pig's heart was stabbed with multiple silver-tipped stakes." The male looked grave. "Just a bunch of haters causing shit." He then turned to Jenna. "You have nothing to fear. We have the situation under control."

She swallowed thickly, nodding once, but her face still looked pale and hers eyes wide.

"It's them." Lazarus' hard eyes landed on him. He kept his comment cryptic not wanting to frighten the little human any more.

"We don't know that," York worked to keep his voice even.

Lazarus snorted. "It's them. I damn well know it is." He moved to the bar gesturing for the barman to give him his weapons.

"Who's them? Is everyone okay? Did anyone get hurt?" Jenna looked panicked. Her heart still raced and she clasped and unclasped her hands.

"A few people in the crowd got splashed by the blood but everyone is fine," the guard said. "It's nothing to worry about."

Jenna nodded again, some of her color returning.

"Can I have a quick word?" He looked pointedly at Lazarus who nodded. They moved to a quieter part of the club. The guards were being questioned and the human females reassured. York hoped that enough of the attention was on other things that no one would be focused on them or their conversation.

"What's up?" Lazarus muttered under his breath.

"I'm leaving."

Lazarus didn't look shocked. His face remained completely neutral. "Are you sure you want to risk everything?"

"I'm just going to talk to her. I need to set the record straight. How did you know that's where I was going?"

"You have a thing for that female."

"I don't," York growled. "Okay maybe I do, but— he shrugged, "it's complicated. I just need to sort things out with her before I can move on. That's all."

"If you go, you will end up fucking her and if you end up fucking her you risk being booted from the program. You need to be very sure that you're okay with that."

Since when had Lazarus turned into a shrink? "I have more willpower than that." York clenched his jaw. "Give me a little more credit."

Lazarus grinned, his teeth gleamed, making him look more murderous than humorous.

"Jeez, bro, don't smile like that around any of the females, they'll run a fucking mile."

His smile widened even further. "Then they must

run. My mate will like that I am built like a brick shithouse, she will love the fact that I drink blood. She will love my smile. When I am with her, I will smile often so she had better love it."

York found himself smiling as well. "You're right my friend. A mate should love everything about you – the good, the bad and the ugly. Even if the ugly outweighs everything else."

His eyes hardened and his mouth became a thin white line. "Are you saying that I'm ugly? I can show you ugly."

"Wouldn't dream of it." York put up his hands, laughing hard. He felt so much better now that he had decided to go and see Cassidy. "I need to get out of here while the attention is diverted elsewhere."

Lazarus shook his head. "Don't say I didn't warn you."

"I'm only going to talk with her."

Lazarus choked out a laugh. "If you say so."

12

CASSIDY LOOKED AT HER bags. They had been packed for days and yet she still hadn't left. Damned if she knew why she hadn't taken the plunge yet.

She'd given notice on the apartment and her lease was paid up. All loose ends had been taken care of. The only thing left to do was to leave. Get in her newly serviced car and hit the road. Destination unknown… the world was at her fingertips with so many opportunities and adventures ahead of her. What the hell was wrong with her?

Right, she was going to shower and hit the sack early so that she could leave in the morning. This was it. Decision made. She waited for the excitement to bubble up inside of her but instead she got… nothing. Not a damned thing. Maybe she was fearful. That was probably it. It wasn't every day a girl got to start over. It was a major life change. It was normal to drag her feet like this. Normal to feel a little apprehensive.

There was a knock at the door.

It must be Mrs. Simmons from next door, she thought. She probably needed to borrow a cup of sugar or some eggs again. The old woman was mostly just really lonely and would make up any excuse to pop in for a quick chat.

"Hi Mrs..." The rest of her words died a quick, horrible death on her tongue, which chose that moment to become paralyzed. Her whole mouth fell open, so the paralysis extended itself to her jaw as well.

He was the last person she had expected to see. York leaned in against the doorjamb. He was wearing a stylish button down shirt and black jeans, sporting a six o'clock shadow that made him all the more attractive. *Bastard!* She didn't want to be attracted to him. It irritated her how his shirt pulled tight across his chest. How his jeans encased thick, mouthwatering thighs. *Damn him!* Cassidy hated the knowing look on his face followed by a half-smile that could ignite panties. Not hers thank you very much. Not again.

She somehow managed to get her mouth to close.

"Can I come in?" Deep and velvety. His voice was like rich, dark chocolate. Melted and dripping in thick rivulets. It made her hungry for things she couldn't have... make that didn't want!

"No." She tried to close the door but he put a boot in the way. "I suggest you move it or lose it." Her voice sounded really confident. *Way to go Cassidy.*

"I need five minutes... please. I need to explain." His eyes shone with sincerity and his voice was filled with remorse.

For a second... just one... she was tempted to let

him in. Then she remembered how he'd used her. Lied to her. Made a fool of her. Her resolve hardened and she shook her head. "Like I said before, I don't want your brand of apology. Please just go away."

His jaw clenched and he sucked in a breath through his nose. For a brief moment it looked as if he was going to back off. Instead, he took a small step towards her, putting him mere inches away.

She had to crane her neck to maintain eye contact. "Go! As in leave... as in turn around and walk away. I'm not interested in what you have to say." *Please go.*

"What Brant said was bullshit! That's not why I went to see you that night." Again, he looked so honest. Like every word was heartfelt. She wasn't buying it. *No way.*

Cassidy shook her head. "Look... I don't know why you're really here, maybe you get off on messing with people's minds or something. Maybe you're some sadistic ass. I don't know. You've said your piece and now you can go."

"You don't believe me," York growled. "I'm not leaving until you hear me out. I'll camp outside this door if I have to."

"Good luck with that since I'm leaving in the morning. My bags are packed and everything," she blurted, feeling like an idiot.

A pained expression crossed his face for a second before he schooled his features. His eyes burned with an intensity that scared her. "I will follow you, Cassidy. Wherever you go. So you might as well hear me out now so that we can both move on."

"That's stalker behavior. You sound like one of

those crazies." *A seriously gorgeous stalker.* In fact, he was the one who should have stalkers, not the other way around.

York smiled and gave a small shrug. "I don't like the way things ended between us. I've done a couple of crazy things since meeting you so one more won't matter." He reached out, almost touching her arm but pulled back at the last second. "I wouldn't be here if I didn't mean it. Why would I care enough? Brant is full of shit. Think about it. Please let me in. I never used you, I swear."

Cassidy rolled her eyes and sighed heavily before looking him in the eyes for a few beats. This was a bad idea but what he said made sense. Why would he care enough to be here if he had used her? Unless he needed something more from her. Maybe he had something else to prove. She started shaking her head.

"I fucking loved our night together," he groaned. "It had nothing to do with the program or Brant or anything else. The only thing that mattered was you... our attraction. The pull I feel for you..." He ran a hand over his head. "I know you feel it too. It's why..." His eyes moved to the side. Someone walked by, slowing down as they neared her door so that they could gawk at what was happening.

Once the person was out of earshot, his eyes moved back to hers. "That's why I'm standing here – like a big loser – at your front door begging to be let in."

"You're not a loser."

"I've never had to beg a female so much in my whole life." He was grinning. "Never." He shook his head. "Maybe I should go." York shoved his hands in his pockets and stepped back far enough to allow her to close the door.

She didn't move.

His eyes softened. Turning from stormy blue to the color of the sky on a sunny day. "I hope you believe me. It was never my intention to ruin your life or to hurt you."

"You didn't ruin my life, that was a bit overdramatic. It did hurt just a tiny…" she held her thumb and index finger a few millimeters apart, "teeny bit to think that you had used me, that's all."

"I didn't use you. I wanted you…" It looked like he wanted to say something more but swallowed the words. His Adam's apple worked. "I'll go now. I'm sure that—"

"Come in," Cassidy interrupted him, stepping back, she held the door open. "Stay for a drink." Her eyes flashed to his. "I have tea, coffee, water… I don't have much I'm afraid," she quickly added, sure to let him know that her blood was not on the menu.

York chuckled. "A coffee would be great." He stepped inside and her small apartment suddenly became even smaller. Then he tensed up and stopped midstride. "Look, I think I should probably go. I said what I needed to say. Damnit, Cassidy…" His eyes lifted to the ceiling for a few beats. "You're beautiful and intelligent. I wanted you more than I've ever wanted anyone. I really hope that you believe that."

When he put it that way, it made her want to jump him all over again but she held back… only just. "I wouldn't have let you in if I didn't believe you."

"Good," his voice was low and deep. It sent shivers

down her spine and had her toes curling into her cheap linoleum floor.

His eyes were so blue, so intense they had her mesmerized. It was then that she realized how close she was to him. Her breath became a little erratic and she swallowed hard. The attraction that flared up between them was so strong that it was practically tangible.

His nostrils flared. "I think I'd better go now."

She felt herself frown. "I thought you wanted a coffee. I can brew us a cup in no time." Cassidy didn't want him to leave... not just yet.

York's nostrils flared a second time and she could see his jawline tense up as he clenched his teeth. He shook his head slowly. "I wasn't lying when I said I wanted you that night."

She could feel how her frown deepened. "I know. I said I believed you."

"I would be lying if I said I didn't want you right now," York whispered. "I think you should ask me to leave now, Cassidy. Kick me the hell out. I'm about to do something we might both regret."

"Oh." Such an eloquent thing to say.

York took a small step back, keeping his eyes on hers. They were burning up with a need that took her breath away.

"Urm..." She wanted him more than she had ever wanted anything before. The problem was that she already had feelings for him after one night. They couldn't be together, so sleeping with him again would only amplify her feelings and hurt her more in the long run.

York gave her a half-smile, actually managing to look forlorn and lost. "All of the best. Don't let some guy mess with you again. You deserve the best, Cass... the best. Don't you dare settle for less."

She nodded, unable to trust her voice.

York turned. Her heart felt like it was beating right out of her chest. "Please, don't go," she whispered.

His whole body stiffened, his neck muscles became distinctly corded. He turned his face ever so slightly. "I should... leave... right now." He sighed. "It's for the best."

"Okay." It came out sounding like a breathless sigh, loaded with disappointment.

"But I can't." He pushed the door shut and turned to face her.

If it wasn't for the desire in his eyes, she would've thought that York was angry. His whole body radiated raw tension. His muscles bulged, straining the fibers of his shirt. He even growled, flashing long, ivory fangs as he advanced on her.

Her heart leapt to her throat and excitement coursed through her veins. He picked her up – as in off the floor – and with no trouble at all.

The little gasp she made was swallowed as his mouth covered hers. His tongue clashed with hers and the sound of ripping filled the room. Cool air abraded her very wet pussy just as his hard cock rubbed up against her. She wrapped her arms around his neck and pulled her knees up.

There was no time to think or even to breathe as her back hit the wall. "Put your legs around my hips. I need to be inside of you." He nipped at her lower lip, sending shock waves through her body. Her clit throbbed. Her breasts felt heavy.

She did as he said, locking her ankles behind him.

"I need you so badly," York moaned as he pushed his hand between them using a finger to rub on her clit. It was at total odds with what he had just said but she didn't care because his touch felt so damned good.

Her breath came in rugged pants which turned to a loud moan when he pushed a finger inside her.

"You're so fucking wet." He cursed in irritation when his shirt tails got in the way of his hand and ripped it open. Buttons went flying, making soft noises at they hit the ground around them. York didn't seem to notice.

It turned her on seeing the desperation etched into his features and actions. This time he breached her with two fingers, pushing in and out of her in slow even strokes that made her cry out.

"Are you ready for me?" he demanded.

She looked down, seeing the head of his thick cock pressed between them. She could feel it hard against her stomach. "Yes." A needy cry was torn from her lips.

York growled, sounding frustrated and he continued to finger fuck her. She could sense that he was holding back.

Cassidy was panting hard. Her orgasm, hovering somewhere just below the surface. "What's wrong? I'm ready."

He groaned again, his eyes went from desire-filled to pained. "I don't want to hurt you. I haven't had sex since I was with you."

And one week without sex was a long time?

Some of the training resurfaced and she remembered them mentioning how sexual vampires were. "Wait a minute." She held onto his hand so that he would stop touching her for a second. "Is that unusual? I mean, is it unusual to go a week without sex?"

York nodded. "Yeah. I'm feeling really turned on right now. I want you so badly... to be inside you... really deep. It's just..." He clenched his teeth and shook his head.

She moved his hand away from her opening and grabbed ahold of his cock. York's eyes drifted shut and he made a growling sound that she'd come to recognize as arousal.

Cassidy closed her hand around his thick girth. "Take me then."

York crouched down a little so that she could position his head at her opening.

"Maybe it would be easier if we went to my bedroom." She licked her lips.

York shook his head. "I'm too desperate for you." He pushed his tip into her.

Cassidy's head rolled back against the wall and she made a whimpering sound.

"Tell me if I'm hurting you," he insisted.

"Feels good," she somehow managed to grind out.

He thrust into her again, deeper this time and she cried out. It stung a little but it mostly felt really fantastic.

"You good?" His eyes were filled with both concern and lust. His jaw was tense, his whole expression told her that he was on edge. His brow was deeply creased.

Cassidy somehow found it in herself to smile. "I won't break. Fuck me already."

It was all that York needed because he shoved her up against the wall with a deep growl. Hard enough to maybe cause a bruise or two, but she didn't care because he thrust into her again and kept on going. Hard and deep. Giving her everything he had. His eyes were locked with hers. He grunted every few strokes. It was cute... it was seriously hot. A sheen of sweat gleamed on his brow. His neck muscles were all over the place.

His dick hit nerve-endings inside her that she never knew existed. She moaned as his pelvis ground against hers, as his hips rocked with hers. As his breath mingled with hers.

"Come for me, gorgeous." York's eyes glowed, while his body demanded. He clenched his jaw and his hands tightened on her.

It was useless to fight it even though she wanted this moment to last. Wanted him joined with her for longer than one more stolen night. In the end, it was useless to hold back.

Everything in her tightened as she felt herself free-fall. Cassidy moaned his name. York jerked against her. She could feel his heat erupt inside of her. He groaned her name as he leaned into her neck.

A pinch.

Blinding pleasure.

A second, even more powerful orgasm was pulled out of her as York clamped down on her neck. She could feel her blood rushing through her veins.

Cassidy sucked in a deep breath and screamed. It felt so good that it almost hurt as her muscles spasmed over and over as wave after wave crashed through her.

Thankfully, he released her within a few hard pulls or she wasn't sure that she would have survived it. It was too powerful, too consuming for a mere human.

Cassidy slumped onto York's shoulder. She couldn't seem to catch her breath.

His chest heaved against hers. Not nearly as labored for the amount of work it must have entailed to have sex with her while holding her up.

Crazy man… vampire. She swallowed hard between desperate pants.

"I'm going to have you on your bed now," York whispered into the shell of her ear, creating goosebumps on her arms and torso and back… hell, the little buggers popped up everywhere.

"Don't you mean take me *to* my bed now?" She sounded ridiculously out of breath. Her voice was a little hoarse from screaming.

He shook his head. "I'm having you *on* your bed." York's eyes were on her lips and he moved forward.

Her eyes were closing in preparation for their kiss when her ringtone sounded. It was shrill because she used one of those cheap throw-away phones.

"I need to get that. It's probably my neighbor."

York moved towards the sound of the phone. Still carrying her. Still inside her. He moved quickly and quietly, putting her down within reaching distance of her phone. Her jeans were still on… sort of. The top part was shredded and hung from her thighs and hips but the pants legs covered her calves and were perfectly intact. She must look really hilarious. Her shirt was still in one piece.

"Hi, Mrs. Simmons." The caller ID showed that it was her neighbor, as suspected.

"Is everything alright, dear?" She sounded really worried.

"Yes, everything is fine." Cassidy swallowed hard when York removed his buttonless shirt, toed off his boots and pulled off his jeans. Naked never looked so good.

No drooling, Cassidy.

"Why did you scream?" Mrs. Simmons didn't sound convinced. "What's going on?"

"I saw a really big spider," Cassidy lied, feeling her cheeks heat. She chewed on her lower lip, letting her gaze move down York's hard body. His dick jutted out from between his hips. Thick and really hard.

"Oh no, dear. That's enough to give anyone a heart attack. How big is it? From your scream, I'm guessing it's quite something."

"You could say that. It's huge." Her voice was a little breathless. "Bigger than I've ever seen before."

A drop of pre-cum beaded on the head of his cock and York grinned.

"Is it one of those really hairy ones?" Her neighbor's voice was animated.

"No, no hairs. Just big and it moves like nobody's business."

His grin widened and he crossed his hands over his chest. The guy was smoking hot. No one had ever made her come so easily. He hadn't even touched her all that much before they had sex. She really needed to get rid of Mrs. Simmons. Cassidy ached for a repeat.

"It's on the move. I need to go," she blurted.

"Be careful, dear. It might be venomous."

Cassidy had to smile. "Although it bites, I don't think it's the venomous kind."

York sniggered, his eyes shone.

"You can't be too careful, Cass dear. Maybe I should pop around and help you with —"

"No need, Mrs. Simmons. I'm capable of taking care of it myself."

"Are you sure?" The old dear still didn't sound convinced.

"Never more sure. You go to bed, it's late."

"Okay." Her neighbor sounded a bit deflated. "Be sure to give it a good clobber with your shoe. Keep hitting until it stops moving."

Cassidy had to cover her mouth with her hand for a few seconds to stop herself from laughing as York covered his dick with both his hands, his eyes were wide.

"I'll be sure to do that." She bit down on her bottom lip when York shook his head, managing to look distraught even though he was grinning broadly.

They said their goodnights and she put down the phone.

"You're not coming anywhere near me with a shoe."

Cassidy pouted. "What if I promised to kiss you better afterwards?"

York choked out a laugh. "What if we skipped the hitting with a shoe part and moved straight to the kissing better part?" He closed the distance between them and picked her up. "Also, your clothes have got to go... I've missed your body."

Her heart skipped several beats, which was stupid since he'd said that he missed her body, not her.

She giggled like a school girl as he practically ran to her bedroom which was the only other room in the apartment. York lay her down on the bed and proceeded to strip her slowly. Her giggles quickly turned to moans when he insisted on kissing every inch of her body until she was writhing and begging for him to take her. When he finally did, it was slow and with infinite care, until she was sure she would self-combust at any second from needing to come.

Just as she was about to all-out beg, he fucked her so hard and fast that her headboard knocked against the wall a couple of times... hell, the whole bed seemed to lift and drop a couple of times. She came hard with York chasing right behind her. He groaned, his body jerked against hers, their loud panting mirroring one another. York seemed to be the type of guy who only allowed himself to let loose when his partner was in the throes of orgasm. Cassidy was shaking by the time he stopped moving, her whole body felt drained of all its energy. Her limbs felt heavy and her eyelids droopy.

He hadn't bitten her this time but it was just as powerful, maybe even more so, since he was on top of her. Their bodies so close that they almost felt like one. *Stop it Cassidy.*

The phone rang and York groaned. It didn't stop him from jumping up and grabbing the device, which he handed to her.

Cassidy pushed the green button. "Hi, Mrs. Simmons." She tried to sound upbeat and awake instead of all drunk on orgasm.

"Did you get him? I heard all the ruckus. You must have got him after all that!" Her neighbor sounded excited.

York's big shoulders shook as he laughed under his breath. The whole bed vibrated, he was laughing so hard.

"Yes, Mrs. Simmons. I sure got him alright."

"Oh good." She sounded ecstatic. Cassidy felt sorry for any critters that ventured into that house. "I'm glad to hear it dear."

"Goodnight, Mrs. Simmons."

"Goodnight, dear."

York wrapped his arms around her and pulled her close. He was still chuckling. "You got me alright," he whispered, almost too softly for her to hear.

It's not what it sounds like, Cassidy. He's referring to sex. Nothing more. When he leaves soon, you will never see him again.

13

6 days later...

LAZARUS SNARLED SO LOUDLY that the human male fell backwards in his haste to get away.

York had to laugh. "You need to stop doing that. This is the only male who agreed to come anywhere near you. A half-finished tattoo is going to look like shit."

"Sorry." Lazarus looked down at the male. "It won't happen again. Silver hurts like a bitch." His face was pinched. His muscles looked strained.

"Stop acting like such a baby." York glanced down at the swirling ink lines on his upper body just above his right pec, it sloped onto his shoulder and lower neck area. His skin was still pink and angry looking from the silver. Lazarus was right though, the silver needle hurt. He was sure that it was from the continuous contact. A quick stab was one thing, ongoing contact got old fast.

The ten males in the breeding program had decided to get inked as a symbol of unity and brotherhood. They had earned their way into the program through courage and brute strength. They were revered by the other males in the covens. Their positions envied. York didn't particularly care either way. It wasn't his idea to get the tat but he agreed to go along with it. The problem was that he wasn't even sure he wanted to be in the program anymore. In many ways, it felt like he was an observer in his life rather than actually living it. The only time he felt truly alive lately was when he was with Cassidy.

"You are thinking about her right now aren't you?" Lazarus asked. The sound of the tattoo gun could be heard buzzing in the background.

York frowned. "I'm not sure who you're referring to. I haven't decided on any of the females yet. We only have to put potential candidates forward tomorrow." He crossed his hands over his chest.

"You may have the rest of them fooled, but not me." Lazarus looked at him through intelligent eyes that saw way too much for his liking.

"I'm not sure what you're talking about."

"You're fucking that human. I can scent human pussy all over you. You scented of it the morning after the meet and greet. The others may have believed your story about how you eased one of the females and how she rubbed herself all over you but I didn't. You forget I know where you went. I still think you're full of shit!" Lazarus said. The tattoo artist stopped working, he looked very interested in what they were saying all of a sudden.

"What the hell are you looking at?" York growled. The human visibly paled. He turned his attention back to Lazarus. "You don't know what you're talking about. There are twenty-five human women currently within the program..." York shrugged. "So I've been screwing around. That's what we're supposed to be doing. It's a breeding program for fuck's sakes. I may have been with *her* that night but not anymore."

Lazarus mouth turned up at the side. "You haven't touched any of the females from the program. You've barely hung around long enough to talk to them. You can count yourself lucky that no one has noticed."

"So I'm discreet. I'm not the type to kiss and tell."

"Yeah..." Lazarus choked out a laugh. "Whatever!"

"I'm done." The tattoo artist looked pale and sweaty. He held out a mirror so that Lazarus could get a good look at his ink. It was a bit more of an elaborate design on the opposite side to York. Same general position. The females would love it... then again, it made him look even meaner.

"Looks good. Thanks." Lazarus rose to his feet and they began walking.

"Don't lie to me, York. You've been disappearing under the guise of fucking one of the humans but you're heading to Cassidy's place. You fucked her that night you left the club and you've been seeing her ever since. Don't even try and deny it."

"Shhh!" York looked around them. "Keep it down. I haven't been fucking her."

Lazarus' face clouded in anger.

York held up a hand. "There's more to it than that. I enjoy being with her." He clenched his teeth for a few beats. "It's not just sex or fucking. I feel like it's… I don't know."

Lazarus cursed. "You're in love with her. I told you to stay away but you didn't listen."

York shrugged. "I'm not sure what to do about it."

"You're getting away with it right now but it's not going to last. Unless you take a human from the breeding program and keep on seeing Cassidy, but I can't see that working."

"I don't know what to do." He felt defeated.

"What has she said about it?"

York shrugged again.

"You guys haven't discussed it?" Lazarus sounded shocked, he raised his brows. "I can't believe you haven't discussed it."

"We're kind of just living in the moment."

"Well it can't last. You're going to get into trouble and I'm talking 'rotting in the dungeon lose your dick' kind of trouble. Thirty lashes will seem like child's play."

York didn't feel like talking about this anymore, he knew he and Cassidy needed to discuss it. He needed to find out her feelings on this. Maybe it was just sex for her. Maybe he was giving up on everything for a female who didn't want him beyond a physical relationship.

"You're right. I'll sort it out. Have you decided who you are going to choose?" The males needed to decide on a female they potentially wanted as a mate. If another male chose the same female, they would be permitted to choose again. It was then up to the males to win their female. Particularly in cases where more than one male chose a certain female. Any males left at the end of the process would get to meet a new batch of females. Any unmated males at the end of three rounds would be scratched from the program.

Lazarus shook his head. "Nah! None of them get me so I'll try again next time round."

"You should try and attend an etiquette class or something."

"A what?" Lazarus frowned.

"It's a class that teaches you how to behave. It teaches manners, which forks to use at the dinner table and how to hold a tea cup." York grinned, sure to let Lazarus know he was joking.

"Fuck forks, fuck tea cups and fuck good behavior! I'm not good... I'm seriously badass and I want a female who will love me for... me."

York laughed. "I'm sure she's out there. I'm not sure that three rounds will be enough to find her though."

Lazarus shrugged. "I hope so but if not then to hell with it. I'm not changing for a female."

"Whatever you say, bro." York shook his head. He for one knew how finding the right female could change a male. How it could turn his perfectly sane world into utter chaos.

Her beautiful eyes brightened as she opened the door. Cassidy threw herself into his arms, wrapping her legs around his hips. Her greeting thrilled him to the core.

It had his dick hardening, downright twitching in his pants. It had been like this every day for the last week. Hard sex followed by fun, easy conversation followed by soft, tender lovemaking that threatened to steal what was left of his sanity. This was very often followed by a call from Mrs. Simmons wanting to know if Cassidy had managed to kill it. As far as Cassidy's nosy neighbor was concerned, Cassidy had a spider infestation.

It made York grin just thinking about it.

"What's so funny?"

"I'm really happy to see you." York said as he kicked the door closed behind him.

"I can feel that." Cassidy nipped at his lip before kissing him quick and deep.

He groaned as she pulled away. "I've missed you." It just slipped out but he couldn't help it, because he meant it.

Her eyes narrowed a tad. "You mean you've missed having sex with me? Twenty-four hours is a very long time." She grinned mischievously.

He could hear how her pulse kicked up a notch or two at the mention of feelings or anything permanent. York groaned softly, feeling how her breasts mashed up against his chest. "Yesterday feels like forever ago. I missed you so damned much." He was talking about her and not the sex – even though he had missed that too. Hopefully she would see his true feelings for her written in his eyes.

Kissing him again, she threaded her fingers through the short hair on his scalp. Her summer dress rode high on her thighs, giving him a glimpse of her stunning legs and the v-neck cut gave him a perfect view of her cleavage. Damn, but she was the most beautiful female he had ever seen.

York tried hard to ignore the packed bags stacked at the entrance to her small hallway. He moved quickly, needing to be inside of her more than he needed his next breath. Within a few strides, York lay Cassidy down on her bed and pulled up her dress so that it bunched around her hips. He couldn't help the low rumble that vibrated from deep inside his chest. "Glistening fucking wet." He dipped his head down so that he could lave her swollen clit. Next, he ran his fingers through the soft fur that had began to grow. "I fucking love your fur."

Cassidy giggled, the sound quickly turned into a drawn-out moan as he sucked on her little bud of nerves. Her fingers dug into his shoulders. He pulled her legs over his shoulders feeling how her toes curled into his back as he continued to suckle on her.

Rainbows and sunshine. Her taste was enough to drive him to distraction. He couldn't help the rumble of satisfaction that moved through him. It didn't take long and Cassidy threw her head back, she grasped the sides of his head with both her hands and gave a raw moan as her back bowed off the bed. In short, she came hard and he loved every drawn out second. Every mewl, every whimper, every pant.

He longed to wake her up like this after a night... together. After they had actually slept wrapped up in each other for the whole night. He longed to slip between her thighs and make her come. Hearing her loud, let-her-rip groan would be the best 'good morning' he could ever hope for. Fuck, any good morning with Cass would be bliss.

All this sneaking around was irritating the crap out of him.

With one sweeping move, Cassidy pulled her dress over her head. "I'm ready for you, big boy."

"I'm not a boy."

"No, but you are damned big." She looked at him from under her lashes. Fuck but she was something.

"No arguments there, gorgeous. Damn…" he let his eyes track the length of her body. "Have I told you today how sexy you are?"

She shook her head, her lip dented as she bit down on it.

"You, my gorgeous female, are so utterly fuckable, it's scary. You might want to call Mrs. Simmons and let her know that you've spotted a big one."

Cassidy giggled while grabbing the bottom of his shirt and yanking it up. He helped her out by lifting his arms. Then she leaned back, her eyes were wide and focused on his chest. "Oh wow!" She gasped. "That's seriously hot."

For a second York wasn't sure what she was talking about, then he looked down. His skin was still a faint pink under the ink. "Oh, this old thing." He tried to play it down, leaning forward to take back her lips but she backed up so that he couldn't reach her.

"It's really pretty," she gushed.

"I fucking hope not," he growled. "Sexy, hot would be fine… pretty…" he snorted. "No… just no."

"Swirling and twirling lines, it looks a bit like an abstract dragon. It is pretty." Her lush mouth pulled into a smile. "In a sexy, hot kind of way."

"When you put it like that…" He reached forward,

wanting to suck on her bottom lip. She had a mouth made for wicked things.

"What made you get it? I didn't even know vampires could have tattoos." Her brow pulled together and the most adorable lines marred her forehead.

York shrugged. "All it takes is a silver needle." His gaze was focused on her mouth... make that her nipples. Utter perfection. Wide areolas and swollen nubs that beckoned him to suck on them and nip at them.

"Ow!! Must have hurt." Her eyes widened. "Let me kiss you better." She kissed him over the tat, somewhere just above his heart. Her soft lips felt like heaven against his skin. "What made you get it?"

"Nothing special," he answered, meaning every word. He really didn't want to have this conversation.

Cassidy frowned. "Why would you get a tattoo for no reason? Go through all that for nothing"

York lifted his brows. "It's nothing. We all got one." He dropped down, taking her nipple into his mouth praying that she would drop it.

Cassidy shrugged him off. "Oh, who's 'we'?"

"The guys." *Leave it the fuck alone.*

"Guys?" Her frown deepened.

"The ten of us." He couldn't say the words.

She sucked in a labored breath and he watched her shut down. Her eyes flashed away from his. Her arm came up across her chest and her mouth tensed. "As in, the rest of the guys enrolled in the breeding program?" It wasn't a question really, but rather a statement.

"Yeah, the dating program." It was his turn to look away.

She let out a shuddery breath. "This isn't… I'm not sure…" Her face took on a pinched look and her eyes still wouldn't meet his.

Fuck!

This was it. The moment he had been dreading. York clenched his teeth so hard that he tasted blood and reveled in it. He'd hurt her… again. At least this proved that she had feelings for him. The knowledge gave him strength for what he was about to propose. She had to buy into it or he didn't know what he would do.

"What the hell are we doing?" she finally blurted. "I should've left town days ago. I mean, are you sleeping with them as well as me?" She made a freaked-out noise. "No, don't answer that. It's none of my business." Her eyes were wide and her lip quivered. A tear tracked down her cheek. He heard her mutter something about the lighting which made no sense to him.

"Please don't cry, Cass." He couldn't stand to see her like this.

She quickly wiped away the tear. "I'm not crying. It's the harsh lighting in here. It always makes my eyes water." She sucked in a deep breath. "Always. I have sensitive eyes." Her voice hitched, belying her emotion.

Using the pad of his thumb, York wiped away the moisture at the corner of her eye. "You can admit that you are crying."

"I'm not damn well crying." She shook her head,

her hair flying about her face.

"I'm in love with you," he murmured, watching as different emotions registered on her face. Shock to elation to pain. It clouded her eyes and pinched her features even more. Another tear tracked down her honeyed skin.

Cassidy swallowed hard, shaking her head. "No, don't say that. We can't be together so it's useless information. It'll confuse things... make things more difficult."

"We can be together," York growled. "We have to find a way. I can see you feel the same about me whether you are willing to admit it or not."

She lifted her gaze and looked him in the eyes for a long while. "It doesn't matter how I feel."

"It does." He took her hand. "I'll get you into the program, Cass. All you have to do is agree. Please."

She shook her head even harder and stood up off the bed before pulling her dress back on. "You have to leave. Go." She pointed in the general direction of the door. When he didn't respond, other than to gape at her, she threw his shirt at him. "Go!" She yelled this time. "You and me are never going to happen. This thing between us is over. It has to be."

York leapt up off the bed and came to land in front of her. Cassidy's expression changed from one of pain to one of shock. Vampires could move pretty fast when they wanted to.

"How can you say that? I just told you that I'm in love with you and I would bet serious money that you feel the same way about me. I'm not going anywhere."

She chewed on her lip, her eyes looked anguished.

"Tell me that you don't feel anything for me and I'll leave…right now."

Cassidy shook her head. "Don't do this. Just go, York." She turned away from him.

"I'll say it again," he let out an exasperated sigh, "I'm not going anywhere, Cass. I'm going to get you into the program whether you like it or not. I'm fucking in love with you and I'm going to find a way to be with you. If you won't fight for us then I'll have to do it for the both of us." York felt desperate. Her reaction told him that she felt the same. Why wouldn't she just admit it?

Cassidy let out a big gust of air. Her eyes were tear-soaked. Her lip actually trembled and he curled his hands into fists wanting to kill the thing that was making her feel this way. Not sure what the hell it was.

A small whimper escaped her and she pursed her lips together for a few beats. "It won't work, York. It just won't work." His name on her lips made him want to fall to his knees in front of her and beg… fucking beg. For all he was worth, and he would gladly do it if he knew it would help.

"You can't know that," he rasped. "We have to at least try."

Her eyes fluttered closed and she put a hand to her forehead. "You don't understand."

"Make me understand, Cass," he growled. "Why is it that I'm willing to fight and you're not? Is this one-sided? Was it just about the sex for you?" He could hear how wounded he sounded and there wasn't a damned thing he could do about it.

"It wasn't just about the sex and you know it!" she

yelled, her eyes on fire with a mix of emotions.

"All I know is that any time I mention something deep or meaningful like how much I've missed you or how I long to wake up with you, you clam up or change the subject. You even turn my words around making them sound flippant. I want to wake up with you... every damned morning. I miss you like hell when I'm away from you for any length of time."

"We hardly even know each other." Her voice sounded incredulous.

"There you go again." It came out sounding gruff. York clenched his jaw, feeling his molars roll together. He tried hard to get a handle on his emotions. "I know you well enough, Cass. I've been with plenty of females and it was never like this. I can't get enough of you and it's only becoming more intense the more time I spend with you. You are 'it' for me."

"No, no..." she repeated the word several times. "This needs to end before..." She let the sentence die.

"Before what, Cass?" He was growling but couldn't help it. "Before what?" he growled again, louder this time when she didn't answer him.

"Before we're in too deep!" Her voice was shrill.

"Too fucking late. I'm already in over my head and so are you. Why are you being so damned stubborn? I want you, Cass... I want us." He cupped her chin, forcing her to look at him. "I want you as my mate." And there it was. Out in the open. All his hopes, dreams, every one of his feelings were on his sleeve. Exposed.

Her heart-rate picked up a whole lot and she licked her lips before sucking in a shuddery breath. "I can't."

It hurt to breathe. His chest ached. "Why? You'd better have a damned good reason."

"I'm infertile!" she all out yelled. Saying the one thing he least expected. Cassidy sniffed, pulling free of his grip. "Don't you see? Your kings would never accept me into their program. I'm broken… flawed. There will be no children's laughter or cute, cuddly babies in my life." Her tears fell freely but she wiped them away with an angry swipe, pulling in a breath which she held deep inside her until the tears stopped.

"Fuck, Cass —" It wasn't the best thing to say in this situation but he was at a total loss.

"I have a really bad form of anovulation. It's normally treatable with drugs but…" She shrugged once, pulling her lip between her teeth. "It didn't work on me. Sean and I tried to conceive for over two years. We had plenty of shitty sex but it didn't help… nothing did. The chances of me ever actually conceiving a baby are almost at zero. I don't ovulate like normal women…" The tears continued to stream down her face. Big drops of pain and anguish. "I don't ovulate, period." Her lashes were soaked. Her nose ran freely. "I even tried fertility drugs, designed to stimulate the ovaries into producing eggs. It was awful…" She continued to cry. "I got hot flashes, bloating and terrible headaches. What I didn't get was pregnant. I can't be with you, York."

"Cassidy," he whispered. It felt like his heart had just been ripped out of his chest. He was in a state of semi-shock. Numbness seeped into him.

What the fuck did he say to that?

How did he make this better?

"I can't join your program!" she yelled, pushing him in the direction of the door. York allowed himself to be shoved. "I can't become your mate. You need to go now!" Her voice was a little hysterical.

York struggled to think coherently. It felt like his whole future had just been snatched away. Another shove and he stumbled in the direction of her front door. "We need to talk about this," he said.

"What's to talk about?" At least her tears had dried up. "Just go, York. Choose one of those women." Her voice hitched. "You and I both know that your uptight king will never allow an infertile woman into the breeding program." She gave a humorless snort. "I can't let you forgo your dreams." Another hard shove and he was outside her front door.

He couldn't recall her even opening it. "Cass, please."

Her face crumbled as she closed the door in his face. He pushed his hands up against the wood. "Let me in." He knocked a few times. "Cass, please. Let's talk about this. This doesn't change my feelings for you. It doesn't change anything."

14

BUILDINGS AND HOUSES SPED by. York had to force himself to take his foot off the gas. To stop at the red light. He gunned it as soon as the light turned green, having to force himself to slow down all over again. His knuckles were white on the steering wheel. Everything inside him was a tense churning mess.

After standing outside her door for at least half an hour, York had finally left. Only because he was afraid one of her neighbors might end up calling the cops. He didn't want trouble for the covens. Not with all the negative press the program had already received.

As he turned onto the open country road, York pushed down on the gas putting Sweetwater behind him.

The longer he had stood there banging on her door, the more he realized that he'd meant every word. He loved Cassidy. It didn't matter that she couldn't bear him children. If his choices were a lifetime with someone he didn't love and a house full of kids or being with Cassidy, there was just no contest. York was hooked on her beautiful smile, her stunning eyes, that splash of freckles over her little nose made something inside of him clench every time he saw them. The sound of her laughter, the softness of her touch... every damned thing about her drove him wild. There was no one else for him.

The Program could go to hell. So could Brant for that matter.

Minutes later, he pulled up to the castle. Parking in a spray of gravel and exiting the vehicle like his butt was on fire.

Someone shouted his name but he ignored it, not even turning to see who needed him. It could all wait.

He made his way down the hall that led to Brant's office. If the male wasn't there, his personal assistant would be able to tell York where he could find his king.

Gideon was in the waiting area. York gave the male a curt nod and walked over to Allison's desk.

The female continued to type at her computer, which annoyed the hell out of him. York put both hands on her desk and leaned in. If this didn't get her attention he'd close her laptop and force her to acknowledge him.

Allison stuck the tip of her manicured nail between her lips and lifted her eyes to him. "Anything I can help you with?"

"I need to see Brant right now... please." He added the last as he watched her eyes widen and her brows lift.

She removed the finger and gave him a regretful

smile. "He is busy at the moment. His schedule is fully booked for the day."

Gideon made a snorting noise. When York looked over at him, he shook his head looking pissed.

"If you're going to insist... like others I know," Allison looked pointedly at Gideon. "You'll need to get in line." She gestured to the seat next to the male.

"All I need is five minutes," Gideon growled, looking agitated, his muscles were bunched, even his hands were fists on his lap. York had never seen him this way.

Allison shook her head, drawing his attention back to her. "No can do. That goes for the both of you..." Her gaze moved back to York. "Come back in," she typed on the keyboard, her face illuminated by the computer screen, "three days. He has a half hour slot at—"

"Forget it," Gideon grumbled. "I'll sit right here until he sees me. In fact..." The male rose to his feet. "I'll go and talk with Zane."

Sheesh, his role as head guard of the program must be taking its toll on him. There were dark smudges under his eyes and they were bloodshot as well. That's when he caught a whiff of Gideon's scent as he brushed past him.

Human.

Too much to just be from casual contact but not enough to be caused from rutting. *What the...* Gideon must have caught his quizzical look because he clenched his teeth. "Don't even go there. It's not what you think."

York put his hands up. "I didn't say a thing. It's

none of my business."

"Damn straight it's not—" Gideon took a step towards the door.

"What are the two of you doing here? You…" Brant half-snarled the word as his eyes narrowed on the other male. "Fuck, Gideon, I gave you my answer yesterday. It's not going it happen. Rules are rules. My answer is still no, so unless you are here for something else I suggest you leave."

Gideon's jaw tensed along with every other muscle in his body. "I was just going." His voice was low and only just shy of a growl. Taking long, fast strides, he left the room.

Brant shook his head. "You had better not be here for anything other than to report on your duties as my *Elite Leader,*" he put emphasis on the words. "Or to tell me how you are struggling to choose between the human females *in* the program because they are all so damn amazing."

York shook his head. "I am here to discuss her."

Brant's eyes turned dark and stormy… as in hurricanes and tornadoes. "I wasn't born yesterday. I know you've been leaving our territory. I know where you've been going," he snorted. "To think I had hoped that you would get her out of your system. I'm a fucking idiot. Get in there!" He gestured inside his office.

"Not the table," Allison called after them. "Try not to hit anything," he heard her add just before the door closed.

"Sit the fuck down!" Brant stormed behind his desk but didn't sit himself. "You had better not be here to ask what I think you are going to ask." He cursed loudly, not giving York a chance to talk. "I'm not bringing her into the program." He paced up and down. "Fuck that, York. It wouldn't be fair of me. It's not fair of you to ask." He ran a hand through his hair. "I should have you flogged, should throw your ass into the dungeon. You don't deserve to be in the program."

He finally stopped pacing and turned to face York, eyes blazing.

York took a deep breath. "Good. We're on the same page then because I want out."

Brant snarled, hitting both his hands on the desk which splintered. The entire structure collapsed in a flurry of papers and files. Brant's computer crashed just to the right of York's foot.

The door opened and Allison put her head around the jamb. She rolled her eyes and sighed dramatically before closing the door.

"Why? You can't have her anyway!" Brant yelled.

"Ross got to have his mate. I want mine. Cassidy is my mate, Brant. I don't care if I have to live in Sweetwater. I don't care if you throw me in the dungeon, it won't change the way I feel about her."

The sound of a ringtone stopped him for a second but when Brant ignored it, York carried on talking. "I love her, Brant. I don't want any other female."

Allison stuck her head around the jamb. "Sorry to interrupt but there is a female at the gate claiming that York will want to see her. She has an expired entry pass. Her name is Cassidy Parker and—"

"Let her in," York instructed, feeling his heart

accelerate and his breath freeze in his lungs and all at the same time. She had come... for him.

Cassidy was here.

Allison turned her gaze to Brant. After several long seconds, his king nodded. "Send her here."

Allison nodded and closed the door.

York let out a ragged breath. "Thank you." He locked eyes with Brant.

"This doesn't mean I'm agreeing to anything." He ran another hand through his hair. His jaw was clenched and his eyes were dark.

After a minute or two, he grabbed his phone and dialed. York could hear Zane answer. Brant relayed the events to the other male.

"I'm kind of busy dealing with an issue," was his cryptic reply. "Whatever you decide is fine with me."

"Fine," Brant ended the call. "Your female must join the program. We need to keep this aboveboard," he growled. "We can't have our males getting funny ideas. We've had protestors at the gate. Just as much bad fucking press as good. We know for a fact that there is a faction out to get the royal family and maybe even the elite in the program. Vigilante shit is not going to fly." He sighed loudly. "Clearly you care too much about this female to let it go."

"She can't join the program," York said, keeping his eyes on the male. "She is infertile."

Brant's face contorted in rage and he cursed a whole string of hard words. "I thought you were desperate to procreate."

York shrugged. "I feel more strongly about her than about having young. I still want her. I love her. I don't care about anything else. Procreation is no longer important to me."

"Are you sure that you want this, because once you are out it's over. I won't take you back."

"I've never been more sure of anything." York could feel himself grinning. He couldn't help it. His female had come to him. It looked as if Brant was about to agree. Things couldn't get much better.

"You can wipe that look off your face," Brant growled. "I don't want to agree to this. I can't believe you males. Why can't you just follow the damned rules?"

York shrugged, keeping his eyes locked with Brant's. "Love doesn't conform. It knows no boundaries or rules... it just is. I love Cassidy regardless of the shit storm it brings down on me. If taking the easy route means that I don't have Cass in my life, then I'll gladly take the difficult path with her by my side. She is mine just as I am hers. There is no other way."

"Oh, York," Cassidy sobbed, drawing his attention to the door. Her eyes were wide and her bottom lip was pulled between her teeth. "Do you really mean it?"

York leapt to his feet so quickly that his chair went crashing. "I'm so glad you came." He ate up the distance between them taking ahold of her hand.

She pulled a little face. "I had to see if you really meant it... about not caring that I can't have kids, that is. I see that it really and truly doesn't matter to you."

York was grinning like the village idiot but he didn't care. He shook his head. "You are all that matters to me, Cass. Only you." He cupped her chin. "I fucking love you." His voice was so deep with emotion.

Cassidy sucked in a breath, her lip quivered. "I love you too. I didn't think it would be possible to fall in love with someone so quickly, but I was wrong." Her eyes filled with tears and she sniffed, clearly trying not to cry. "I know you well enough to know that you are 'it' for me too." A single tear fell and he was just about to wipe it away and kiss the hell out of her when Brant interjected.

"Hold on just a damned minute," he barked, standing right next to them. "I haven't given permission for the two of you to be together. You are still officially a part of the program." His hard gaze bore into York.

He didn't give a damn what Brant said, or what Brant wanted. His king could go fly a kite right off a tall cliff for all he cared. He and Cassidy were going to be together. York had meant what he said about leaving if he had to.

Brant cursed. "You are, unfortunately, right about love not damn well conforming to rules." He shook his head. "Even when those rules are for the best. The thing is, I do understand... I really do. I've become such a fucking wimp since Sam was born... hell... since Tanya came into my life." His whole demeanor softened. His eyes radiated love.

It was the strangest thing York had ever seen. The male standing in front of him right now was not his king. It was like aliens had invaded Brant's body. York held his breath. Cassidy's focus was solidly on Brant as well. She too seemed to be holding her breath.

"I'm probably going to regret this, but I hereby expel you from the program." Brant looked pointedly at York. "Your female is welcome to join the coven."

York was about to fist punch the air when Brant carried on talking, making him suck back a breath into his lungs.

His king turned to face Cassidy. "You do realize that when a vampire mates, that it is for life? There is no going back… no divorce, no fucking around with other males. We are *not* humans and you need to be very sure that this is what you want. If you mate one of ours, you will become one of us, governed by our lores and a part of our ways. Do not take this decision lightly."

"I'm sure," Cassidy shrieked. She threw herself into Brant's arms. "Thank you so much. You won't regret this."

Oh shit!

Cassidy was so excited that she was hugging Brant. Hugging the meanest motherfucker ever to walk the earth. Blood had been shed, in the past, over less. At first, his king just stood there like a statue. Then he shook his head and actually smiled. Brant smiled. It was a small miracle. He put one hand lightly to Cassidy's back and sort of hugged her back.

York had to chuckle. Everything was coming together. Then Brant's face took on a confused look and a frown appeared on his forehead. "What is the meaning of this?" he demanded.

Cassidy jumped back, making a soft gasping noise. York pulled her behind him, putting himself between his female and his king. He couldn't help it when his hands squeezed into tight fists.

"Why the fuck would you lie?" Brant snarled. "What purpose could it possibly serve?"

"My lord?" York didn't know what his king was referring to.

"This female is not infertile." Brant's eyes were narrowed and his fists clenched.

It was York's turn to frown. He glanced over his shoulder at Cassidy who looked just as shocked and confused as what he felt.

"Scent her," Brant growled, gesturing in Cassidy's direction. "If she's infertile then I have a tiny dick." He made a snorting noise.

York turned, yanking Cassidy into his arms. She gasped but didn't try to pull away when he buried his nose into her neck. He sniffed deeply.

Fuck!

York made a growling noise. His cock instantly hardened and his heart-rate picked up. Adrenaline surged. His first reaction was to throw his female over his shoulder and to find the nearest quiet spot in order to completely ravage her. He resisted – only just. "That smells so damned good." His voice sounded thick to his own ears.

"What does?" Cassidy pushed at his chest. "What's going on?" She licked her lips, her beautiful eyes were wide and a little fearful.

"Um… Cass…" York grinned. "Would you like to get pregnant?" Excitement coursed through him.

Confusion and pain warred with her delicate features. Her eyes clouded and a deep frown took up residence on her face. "Don't say that. I would love to have a child but I told you that I can't. I don't ovulate. Even the strongest fertility drugs didn't work. Please, York, don't say things like that, it isn't fair." Her lip wobbled.

Brant chuckled. "All I can say is that we have the most potent fucking seed."

York ignored his king and cupped Cassidy's chin. "I would never do such a thing. You are at the start of your heat. I couldn't pick it up earlier and it is barely there now, but it's happening…" He couldn't help but smile.

Her confused expression became even more pronounced. "I don't know what you are talking about. What the hell is heat? It's really hot outside but I don't know what that has to do with me or babies."

Brant had walked over to his wrecked desk and was rummaging through the debris. He gave another small chuckle. "Hot outside," he muttered while shaking his head.

"Don't look so worried." York cupped her face in both of his hands. "You are going into the fertile part of your cycle."

"I don't have a fertile part of my cycle. I don't have a cycle, period." She tried to pull away from him. "Stop this crazy talk."

"Hold still." He moved his hands to her hips, holding on so that she couldn't get away. "Brant and I can scent that you are preparing to release an egg. We call it 'going into heat' and you humans call it ovulate."

Cassidy narrowed her eyes, still frowning. "Don't

you mean ovulation?"

"Yeah, that's exactly what I mean."

"Wait a minute. Are you saying that you can smell on me that I'm about to ovulate?"

York nodded. "Yeah, it is a unique and wonderful scent that cannot be missed. It makes me want to rut you right now."

"This is my office!" Brant yelled. "Don't even think about it."

York continued to ignore his king, his sole focus was on the female in front of him. *His female.* Her frown eased. He could see that she was thinking things over. The edges of her lips curled upwards in the start of a smile. "Are you sure?" Her words were breathless.

"Very sure, Cass. You will be fertile over the next few days. We might be able to have a baby." His heart was racing about a mile a minute. He clenched his jaw, feeling a well of emotion rise up inside of him. The thought of having a child with this amazing female did strange crazy things to him.

Her pulse took off and her breathing became a little erratic. It looked like she might have a panic attack or something. Her gaze dropped and then fixed on the ground. He couldn't get a handle on what she was feeling or thinking.

"That is... if you want to try," he said. "We don't have to. It's just that it might not happen again and right now there's a good chance that—"

"I want a baby." When she looked up, her eyes were tear-soaked and this time judging from her wide smile, it was out of sheer happiness. Her eyes sparkled and she even gave a small bounce.

"Are you serious?" York asked, feeling like an idiot for even asking.

"Yes, I am." Dents appeared in her lower lip when she bit down on it.

"Are you sure? It's a big step and — "

"I'm so very sure. I want a baby!" She made an excited noise. "Let me rephrase that, I want a baby with you, York. I couldn't think of anything better." Her eyes were locked with his. They shone with sincerity.

"We're back in the program." York flicked a glance at Brant who was trying to get his computer to work.

"Fuck that," Brant growled. "I said you were out, so you're out. I told you that there would be no coming back."

"I don't give a flying fuck about the program... I love you, Cass." He closed his lips over hers, swallowing her reply.

By blood, she tasted better than anything he had ever experienced. His cock twitched as her tongue swirled with his. Her hands came up around his neck and her breasts pushed up against him.

York growled, pulling her more firmly against him. He palmed her lush ass with both his hands.

"Get a damn room," Brant mumbled, reminding York that he was still in his king's office. The only thing on his mind right now was being inside of his female. Making babies. He grinned at Cassidy as he pulled away from her and she grinned back.

"Are you okay with moving in with me?" He had to double-check that she was comfortable with moving to the castle.

She started to nod when Brant spoke. Cassidy's eyes stayed on York.

"I'll organize you one of the bigger suites. A single room is no place to raise a child."

Just the thought of Cassidy's belly swelling with his child had a lump forming in his throat.

"Let's go and fetch my bags," she giggled softly. "I'm already packed."

York leaned in so that his lips brushed against her ear. He felt her shudder, loving that he had that effect on her. "You do realize that we're going to have to make love many, many times over the next few days?"

"Oh, I really hope so," she gushed, and he could hear that she was smiling. "Let's go fetch my bags then."

"We might be a little while." York managed to tear his eyes off of Cassidy long enough to glance at Brant.

"Sweetwater is only fifteen minutes away," Brant said. Then he chuckled. "Go and fetch your soon-to-be-mate's bags. Let them know at the gate that you will be gone for a few hours."

"The rest of the day," York's voice had turned husky but that wasn't to be helped.

"Fine," Brant growled louder this time. "Just get the fuck out of my office already. I'm going to have to make an example or two around here to stop this shit from happening again." He shook his head, pretty much talking to himself. "I've had it with insubordination."

Brant wasn't as bad as he made out to be. He had gotten to know the male well over the years. Although he could be a cruel, soulless motherfucker at times, he was that way because he cared. The key was to make sure you were with him. Get on his bad side and you were screwed – good and proper.

York grabbed Cassidy's hand and walked out before his king could change his mind. Full moon couldn't come soon enough and until then, he was going to work hard on filling her belly with his seed. He couldn't wait to get started.

15

THEY RUSHED UP THE stairs and down the hall. Cassidy could see her apartment just up ahead. York kept squeezing her ass and trying to touch her and kiss her. She slapped his hand away for the tenth time since they'd exited the vehicle.

Cassidy giggled. "Stop that. I can't find my keys." She rummaged around in her purse.

"I can't wait to have you," he rumbled, sending shivers up and down her spine.

Just as her hands closed on the set of keys, there was the sound of someone clearing their throat. York took a small step away from her which was strange since he was so damned big and strong. Who could possibly have caused such a reaction in him?

Cassidy whipped her head to the side and there stood dear old Mrs. Simmons, looking anything but sweet and frail. Her arms were folded across her chest and her foot tapped a fast, even beat on the floor. The noise echoed through the hallway. Her eyes were narrowed and blazing. "I thought you'd taken care of that spider problem. You told me you had them exterminated." She said the word with such venom that York actually flinched.

"Um... no, no extermination. Just a little misunderstanding. It turns out I really like spiders after all... very much."

"You're sure it's not venomous? Those poisonous ones are real pests. Deserve to be squashed, the lot of them." To emphasize a point, she bent down and removed her shoe, whacking it on the wall with a loud crack, she even glanced at York as the shoe hit home.

York moved back in next to her and even put his arm around her. "Deservedly so."

Cassidy put a hand out to touch the old woman's arm. "Thanks for your concern. I'm fine, better than fine. There is no need for extermination services, I assure you." She smiled at her soon to be ex-neighbor, who did visibly relax – at least to a degree. "I'd really like for you to meet my fiancé, York."

Mrs. Simmons gave him the once-over. "Well alright then, but don't hesitate to call if you need to borrow a shoe." She still ignored York, as well as the fact that she'd just introduced him as her fiancé. Her heart raced and she couldn't help the smile that took hold of her mouth at the mere thought of becoming his wife... mate. A much better concept.

"It's really good to meet you, ma'am. I promise to do right by Cassidy. I love her very much." Her heart ached when she saw the emotion reflected in his eyes.

Mrs. Simmons must have seen it too because she finally relaxed completely and even smiled at York.

"Good, she hasn't had it easy and deserves a good man to take care of her. You are a fine specimen, aren't you?" Then she was looking him up and down like he was a hot chocolate sundae on legs.

York gave one of his gorgeous panty-combusting half-smiles. "I will take excellent care of her, I promise."

"Just one more little thing." The old lady turned to Cassidy, putting a hand up around her mouth to block what she was saying from York. As if that was even possible. Keeping her voice really low, Mrs. Simmons leaned in. "I believe you said that the spider was hairless. Did you mean it?" Her eyes were wide, they glinted mischievously.

Cassidy felt York twitch behind her, obviously trying to keep from laughing. Biting down on her lip, Cassidy had to work hard herself. "We have to go, Mrs. Simmons. Take care of yourself." Before her neighbor could say anything more, she inserted the key in her door and they both flew inside closing it behind them. Cassidy had to put her hand over her mouth to hold back a laugh. It threatened to spill right out. York's great, big shoulders shook and his eyes filled with tears but he didn't make more than a soft grunting sound.

"She's something," he finally choked out.

"She's harmless."

"And really sweet. Good thing I plan on loving you always or I would be really scared." His eyes were locked with hers. Blue like a crystal spring.

"Good thing," she whispered.

His chest still heaved from holding back his

laughter, his eyes narrowed on her, turning hungry and desire-filled. His nostrils flared. They reached for each other at the same time.

His fingers dug into her flesh just as hers clasped his. York growled; it was loud and quite terrifying. If she wasn't used to the noises he made, she would be very afraid right now. Her heart raced and her skin felt flushed but not from fear. The opposite was true.

"I want you so badly. The scent of your heat is getting stronger." His eyes moved from her lips back to her eyes and back to her lips again. His irises glowed. His skin was taut and all of his muscles were bunched. "I need you wet, Cass." He pushed a hand under her dress and ripped off her panties. Shredded them like they were paper.

It turned her on big time and she gave a little squeal. Then his fingers found her clit and the squeal turned into a moan.

"That feels good," she panted, as his other hand palmed her breast.

"I need to see you," he groaned, tearing the front of her dress with a loud rip. His gaze dipped to her chest and he made a sound of annoyance, snapping the front of her bra using just his fingers.

His features relaxed somewhat. "Much better." He picked her up easily, closing his hot mouth over one of her hardening nubs.

Cassidy put her legs around him. Her clit throbbed and she rubbed her core against him as her ankles locked at his back.

"I can't believe it," she said the words that had been swirling around in her head on the whole trip over here. "We're going to be together."

"You had better believe it." He lowered her and nipped her lip before swirling his tongue with hers.

"Are we really trying for a baby?" she asked as he broke the kiss. "Because I can't believe that either."

"We will be trying very hard and very often. Your scent is getting stronger by the second. There is no doubt that you are fertile. I'm not sure how it happened but it has and we are going to make the most of it." He began to move taking long, easy strides. "I'm going to rut you on the bed now."

"Mmmm, the bed." She ground herself up against his erection.

York groaned at the contact, nipped at her ear. "The bed... the shower... the floor... the wall... the kitchen...everywhere." Each word came out on a rough pant. "The heat can get pretty hectic; your scent is going to drive me insane with need. You need to be prepared, Cass." He suddenly looked worried.

"What?"

He deposited her carefully on the bed. "There are some things you should know about a vampire pregnancy. You need all the facts before we do this. I can't believe I didn't think to tell you before. I was too damned happy."

"It doesn't matter. I want this."

He shook his head. "Hear me out first."

Cassidy nodded. There wasn't much he could say that would put her off this.

"You will be pregnant for a whole year. We were briefed that human pregnancies only last nine months." He looked so worried that she had to lean forward and kiss him softly on the lips.

She moved back slightly, keeping them nose to nose. "I will happily carry your child for a whole year." She moved back a bit more. "As long as you promise to give me lots of back rubs."

York smiled, looking so damned handsome it threatened to take her breath away. "That's a deal."

"Besides," she bobbed her eyebrows up and down, "pregnant women are supposed to be extra horny, so we can have loads of sex."

His face looked pained for a moment and he moaned. "No, don't talk about sex... I need to get through this conversation and your scent is making it impossible as it is." He paused, readjusting his cock before continuing. "Um... sheesh..." He rubbed his hand over his head. "As a human, you might not like this one..."

"Try me."

York looked her deep in the eyes. "If you can't do it then I will understand."

"Tell me." She narrowed her eyes at him.

"You will get thirsty." He raised his brows. "As in very thirsty."

She could see that there was more. When he didn't say anything more she prompted him. "Thirsty is no big deal. What kind of thirsty?" She could guess.

"For blood, Cass. You will need to drink from me often."

Cassidy had to smile at him. "I already bite you all the time during sex."

His face got this goofy, faraway look. "I love it when you do that. Makes my dick fucking explode." He turned serious. "Blood drinking is a whole other level."

"If I drink from you, will it be as good as when you drink from me?"

He nodded, his eyes glowed softly and his nostrils flared. "Big time. Mated couples drink from one another, it is the vampire way."

"I'm going to be your wife... your mate. I want you to be satisfied. I won't lie, the thought freaks me out a little but I'm good. I'm sure I'll love it."

York swallowed thickly. "I love you, Cass. I can't wait to be inside you so I'm going to move onto the next thing now because I don't have much patience left."

"There's more?" She quickly smiled to show that she was joking... well sort of joking.

York nodded. "Your breasts will fill with blood instead of milk."

Cassidy shrugged. "That figures. I would give birth to a vampire baby so it stands to reason that he or she would drink blood."

"He," York said.

Cassidy felt herself frown. "What do you mean by he? He as in a boy? You can't know that."

"The child will be a boy. We are not sure why but all vampire/human births to date have led to the births of boys. We will have a son."

"A son. I don't want to get too excited yet. What if I don't get pregnant?" It felt like a boulder landed in the pit of her stomach. To think just hours earlier she had thought she would never conceive, never be a mom, never get to experience the wonderful gift of giving life to another.

York cupped her chin. "Then we will try again and again and keep going until it happens. It will happen, Cass, of this I am sure."

She nodded, trying hard to believe him. Wanting so badly for it to be true.

York grinned, letting his hand fall away. "Vampires have seriously potent seed and as the Elite Leader, my sperm is particularly powerful."

Cassidy had to laugh, she shook her head. "I'm sure you're right. Is there anything else I should know?"

York clenched his jaw, his eyes darkened up. "It is not without risk. My kings almost lost their mate early on in her pregnancy. Human females will struggle to survive a miscarriage. Even our own females are greatly affected. The good news is, you will become stronger and even take on some of our vampire traits, not just blood drinking but general stuff."

"Like what? How soon?"

"It will happen after we mate and will gradually become more pronounced as we bond with one another. You drinking my blood will strengthen the bond between us." His eyes lightened as a hunger returned. "You will see better, hear better, all of your senses will become magnified. You will age slower..."

"If I had known that, I would've agreed to this much sooner. In fact, I would've joined the breeding program instead of the trial phase," Cassidy joked.

York frowned, his whole body became tense.

"What is it? I was only joking." She moved closer to him, grabbing his biceps.

When he locked eyes with her, he smiled. "I know

that." He kissed her. A quick brush of the lips. "I told you that I've never had to work so hard to get a female as what I had to with you. Almost impossible." His face became serious and his jaw tensed. "It's just that there are females within the program for the wrong reasons. You just reminded me of that."

"What? Women who want to slow down aging?"

"I hadn't thought of that one since it is not a major thing for vampires, but yeah. There are more advantages to being with us; they want money, and to live in luxury. I worry that a male might end up with someone like that."

"Give the guys some credit." Cassidy pulled her shredded dress over her head and shrugged out of the ruined bra. "I'm sure they're more intelligent than that."

"Sometimes a male will lose his mind," he spoke slowly, his eyes on her breasts. York growled softly, sending a shiver up her spine.

"Was there anything else you needed to tell me?" Her pussy felt slick. Her nipples pebbled under his scrutiny.

He shook his head. "More than likely but damned if I can remember." His nostrils flared and he licked his lips. "I think I covered the important stuff." His eyes drifted to the juncture of her thighs. "I want you on your hands and knees, Cass. Since you are about to become a vampire's mate, I need to rut you... seriously rut you and in true vampire style."

"Have you been holding back?"

York shook his head. "There is no such thing with you. I couldn't if I tried." He pulled his shirt over his head, tossing it on the floor.

His words warmed her.

"Do you need to let Mrs. Simmons know that you are about to see a whole damn horde of spiders?" He kicked off his boots and lost his jeans in record time.

"More like one really big, hairless one." She looked down. His magnificent cock jutted from between his hips.

York's gaze turned feral and his eyes glowed, his cock actually twitched. "I hate to tell you, gorgeous, but you're not going to be seeing much of my cock..." He palmed his thick girth. "It's going to be buried too deeply inside of you for you to see much of anything." He winked at her.

If she wasn't wet before, that changed now. Just hearing him talk of sex with her had her breathing turning a little ragged.

"On your knees, gorgeous. I need you to hold on tight." He gave her a wicked grin. "Making babies is serious business."

Cassidy moved onto all fours, sure to poke her ass up in the air. She widened her stance, feeling the air abrade her inner thighs and sensitive flesh.

"You are so beautiful. I'm going to last all of five seconds," York growled.

"I doubt that," she groaned as his tongue breached her opening. She cried out when its long length vibrated inside her, as he made a low rumble of pleasure.

"So good," he groaned as he moved to her clit. He closed his mouth over her and sucked, making her gasp. His tongue swirled around and around against her bundle of nerves until she was rocking against him. Her heavy pants turned to even heavier moans.

Just as her pussy began to flutter, York pulled back. "I can't be gentle," a whispered growl, as he crouched over her, his chest against her back. York grabbed her hips, holding on tight. She might have bruises in the morning but right now she didn't give a shit.

A shrill cry was torn from her as he thrust into her in one hard move.

York grunted loudly, staying perfectly still for a few beats. His chest heaved and his breath came in ragged pants. He kissed her on the side of her neck. "Are you okay?"

She could barely understand him, his voice was so deep and guttural. It made her even hotter for him. "Yes," she moaned.

He pulled out slowly and carefully until just the tip of his cock was inside of her. "Good," York grunted as he thrust back into her.

He fucked her hard and slow. Her whole body shook with each deep thrust. The bed lifted and landed. The headboard knocked. It was hard to breathe, impossible to think. She could only feel. York's hands were on either side of her. His hot breath on her neck. On and on… thrust after thrust.

Her breasts were smashed against the mattress. Her arms shook from clinging to the covers. Her orgasm snuck up on her. It felt good one second and then her back bowed and her eyes closed. A deep, raw groan escaped as her pussy began to spasm. Her orgasm flashed awake inside of her somewhere deep in her belly. It then seeped through every part of her like a thick, spreading warmth.

When York bit down on her neck, she screamed. The pleasure so intense, it had her seeing fireworks. Which was weird since her eyes were closed.

He grunted and then all out moaned as his movements became jerky. Cassidy could feel his warmth spurt deep inside her. Then he slumped on top of her, careful not to squash her. He was breathing hard.

With a soft moan, he rolled to his side taking her with him, their bodies still joined. His arm wrapped around her and his hand clutched her stomach. His fingers began to trace the skin on her belly with a softness that warmed her heart.

They had a ton to look forward to. Just thinking about it made her smile. Cassidy sighed, snuggling closer to the vampire curled behind her. *Her vampire.*

16

His ARMS WERE FILLED with softness. The scent of sunshine and rainbows filled his nostrils. York couldn't help but groan as he pulled Cassidy closer. From the feeling of warmth on his skin, he guessed that the morning was well on its way.

He snuggled into the crook of her neck, nipping at the sensitive skin there.

It was Cassidy's turn to moan. She stretched out, stifling a yawn. "You've worn me out." Her voice was still thick with sleep.

His heart filled with warmth. It was the fourth day he was waking up with her and he loved it just as much as he suspected he would. Hugging her even closer, he whispered into her ear. "I told you that the heat could get pretty hectic."

She made a little snorting sound. "I think I might need a band aid for my lady bits."

York couldn't help but laugh. "No need, I will kiss you better."

The scent of her arousal filled the air and York had to grin. They had made love countless times over the last few days. He still didn't have his fill of her, although he suspected that he never would. Even a lifetime was too short.

"Am I still in heat?" Cassidy turned her head, so that her wide eyes met his.

York shook his head. "No." His gaze dropped to her breasts, which had come into view as she turned. He dipped his head and sucked on her nipple. So tasty and just so damned arousing, his already hard cock began to throb.

Cassidy looked a little crestfallen. "So..." She paused for a long while and he released her nipple with a soft popping noise.

"What is it?" York was sure to look her deep in the eyes.

Cassidy shrugged. "I'm just a little nervous. I really want to be pregnant. I only hope we made love enough times."

Although this was a serious moment, he had to chuckle. "I think we have that covered. My balls have actually shrunk in size." He planted a kiss on her temple.

She gave a breathy sigh and he noticed that her hand dropped to her belly. "I just want this so badly, York." She licked her lips. "We'll know in a few days, right?"

He cupped her chin, reveling in the soft skin under his hand. "Yeah, it won't take long. You'll develop a thirst that just won't quit no matter how much you drink. The queen informed me that your little canines will sharpen and extend. They will still be very small, unlike our fangs." He curled his lip away, allowing his teeth to extend.

Her eyes widened and again her arousal blossomed.

York fucking loved how his vampire side turned her on.

"You will start to crave blood and will only be satisfied once those little fangs are firmly in my neck and my blood is on your tongue."

Although she pulled a face, he could see that she wasn't nearly as grossed out at the prospect as most humans would be.

Cassidy looked down at the bed, her eyes were clouded in worry.

"Hey." York put a hand around her waist. "I will be there for you every step of the way. It's not as bad as you think. I have a feeling that you will take to it quickly and easily."

Her green-tinged eyes met his. "That's not it," she all but whispered. "I'm just so worried that I'm not... you know... pregnant. I want this so badly for you... for us."

"We will try again, Cass. I for one, will love every minute of every heat you have."

"I might not have another heat." Her lip quivered. "It's a miracle I ovulated this time. I still can't believe it."

"Firstly, vampire seed is potent... as in ridiculously so. All females who are not capable of birthing young—" Best to explain that, just in case no one else had. "Most of our females have pelvises that are too narrow to be able to birth young. Cutting the child out is impossible because a silver blade would need to be used and silver is toxic to infants."

"And here I was feeling jealous of their narrow hips." A look of guilt crossed her face.

"You don't have to feel guilty, but you certainly don't have anything to feel jealous over either. Most of our females would kill to have hips like yours." He clasped her there, feeling her soft flesh beneath his fingers. "You have no idea what your lush curves will do to a male."

She giggled. "Actually, I think I might have a small inkling." Her heated gaze dropped to his cock, which twitched under her scrutiny.

"My greedy little female. I'm not finished with this conversation, but I need you to hold onto that dirty thought."

Her eyes lifted and locked with his.

"Females who can't birth young have themselves sterilized, because even though we can scent when a female is in heat, mistakes can happen. Even when being extremely careful. When males rut their mate during the heat, it almost always results in the female becoming pregnant."

Cassidy nodded. "I'm still nervous. I just want this so much. It's your greatest desire to become a dad and I want you to have that." She bit down on her lower lip and her eyes filled with tears.

It killed him to see her like this.

"I have exactly what I want. That's you, Cass. You are my greatest desire." The pad of his thumb trailed along her jawbone.

She smiled and a tear streaked down her cheek. "Do you really mean that?"

"Fuck, yes. I am already the happiest male on earth. Even if we never have a baby, I am truly satisfied and completely fulfilled because we have each other."

Another tear tracked down her cheek and he wiped it away. "Please don't cry."

Her smiled widened and her eyes sparkled. "I'm not crying," she sniffed. "It's the harsh morning sun. I have sensitive eyes." Cassidy giggled softly.

York had to shake his head, making sure to give her a look that told her she was full of shit. "Now," he growled while pulling her against him. "About that wicked thought you had earlier."

Her giggle grew louder. It was in that moment that York knew, without a single doubt, that they were going to be just fine regardless of what happened.

A Mate for Gideon is available now.

AUTHOR'S NOTE

Thank-you for reading the first in this series.

If you want to be kept updated on new releases please sign up to my Latest Release Newsletter to ensure that you don't miss out —

www.mad.ly/signups/96708/join

I promise not to spam you or divulge your email address to a third party. I send my mailing list an exclusive sneak peek prior to release. I would love to hear from you so please feel free to drop me a line —

charlene.hartnady@gmail.com.
Find me on Facebook —
www.facebook.com/authorhartnady

I live on an acre in the country with my gorgeous husband and three sons and an array of pets including a couple of horses.

In my spare time you can usually find me typing frantically on the computer completely lost in worlds of my making. I believe that it is the small things that truly matter, like that feeling you get when you start a new book or a particularly beautiful sunset.

BOOKS BY THIS AUTHOR

The Chosen Series:
Book 1 ~ Chosen by the Vampire Kings
Book 2 ~ Stolen by the Alpha Wolf
Book 3 ~ Unlikely Mates
Book 4 ~ Awakened by the Vampire Prince
Book 5 ~ Mated to the Vampire Kings (Short Novel)
Book 6 ~ Wolf Whisperer (Novella)

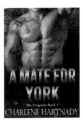

The Program Series (Vampire Novels):
Book 1 ~ A Mate for York
Book 2 ~ A Mate for Gideon
Book 3 ~ A Mate for Lazarus
Book 4 ~ A Mate for Griffin
Book 5 ~ A Mate for Lance
Book 6 ~ A Mate for Kai
Book 7 ~ A Mate for Titan

BOOKS BY THIS AUTHOR

The Bride Hunt Series (Dragon Shifter Novels):
Book 1 ~ Royal Dragon
Book 2 ~ Water Dragon
Book 3 ~ Dragon King
Book 4 ~ Lightning Dragon
Book 5 ~ Forbidden Dragon

Demon Chaser Series (No cliffhangers):
Book 1 ~ Omega
Book 2 ~ Alpha
Book 3 ~ Hybrid
Book 4 ~ Skin
Demon Chaser Boxed Set Book 1–3

A MATE FOR GIDEON

The Program Book 2

CHARLENE HARTNADY

1

LIAM'S HANDS WERE WHITE-KNUCKLED on the steering wheel. Other than that, he was the picture of calm. He hadn't said a word to her since leaving the barbecue. Hadn't so much as looked in her direction.

Jenna kept her hands folded in her lap and tried to keep her eyes on the road ahead. She couldn't help but sneak the odd little glance in his direction every now and then, out of the corner of her eye. Maybe she was misreading the signals.

Please let her be misreading the signals. *Please.*

Sucking in a breath through her nose, she

swallowed thickly. Who was she kidding? If Liam was giving off any kind of signals, trouble was just around the corner. She knew that there was nothing she could do to avoid the inevitable. To think that she had tried so hard today. She had worked at being nice, but not overly so. Maybe she hadn't been nice enough? Was that it?

Every so often she would go over to Liam and hold his hand or offer to refresh his drink. She'd even fetched his dinner for him. If she'd been any more attentive than she already was, it would've meant getting down on her knees and sucking him off right there in front of everyone. More, she could not have done. Could she have?

As much as she wanted to feel anger, she couldn't, she was too scared. The emotion rolled around inside of her and turned her stomach to knots. Her armpits were damp and a bead of sweat trickled between her breasts. Her mouth felt so dry that her tongue stuck to the roof of it. It was a feeling she knew well. It lived inside her. Had done so for so long that it had become a part of her. Yup, she and fear were great friends. In fact, fear was the only friend she had left.

The car pulled into their drive and the garage door slowly opened. Liam let out a sigh as they drove in, the garage door closed behind them with a clunk. Then there was silence.

Not sure what to do next, Jenna unclipped her seatbelt, opened the door and slipped out of the car. She moved to the rear of the vehicle where she opened the backdoor and retrieved her empty salad dish. It had been her contribution to the barbecue. The dish shook in her hand, threatening to fall, so she clasped it to her chest. Liam was already out of the car and making his way to the door that led to the house.

She was too afraid to look in his direction. Too petrified to talk. If she said the wrong thing it could spark his mean streak. She'd learned very quickly that there were three sides to him, mean, meaner and the side he showed the rest of the world. That side of him was charming, attentive, attractive. Liam had a lean swimmer's build and preppy good looks. Even the women at today's barbecue had gushed when he'd taken his shirt off and delivered one of his killer smiles. It was only she who knew how killer that smile really was.

She swallowed hard.

His gun was in the safe in their bedroom. The knowledge burned inside her and made her gut churn faster. Her mouth felt dry. Her tongue stuck to the roof of her mouth even more.

Liam turned the light on and then stopped dead as they walked into the kitchen. Jenna was so busy staring at her feet that she nearly crashed into his broad back. She lifted her head, having to crane her neck to see the back of his head. All she had was a partial side view. Damn, his jaw was clenched. Oh god, he was a big guy. It was one of the things that had attracted her to him in the first place. His height, his dark hair, he looked a lot like… *Not going there. Not right now.*

Her lip quivered as she tried to force a smile. "Can I get you something to eat?" Stupid thing to ask after they had just got home from a barbecue, but she had no idea what else to say. She put the bowl down on the nearby counter. He would only get angrier if she accidentally broke it. Liam hated it when she was clumsy. Anything could set him off. By the tension that radiated from him now though, it was too late to try to stop this.

"A drink maybe? I could put the kettle on…" Her voice shook just a little, belying her fear.

"Shut the fuck up," he spoke softly, still facing away from her. For the longest time he didn't say anything more.

Jenna had to work not to squirm or to move away. Neither of those things would help her. In fact, they'd only make it worse. What had she done wrong? Maybe she hadn't done something she should have? Jenna wracked her brain, coming up short.

"I can't believe you," he finally said, shaking his head and turning to face her. Anger made his eyes blaze and his fists curl. His brow furrowed and his jaw tightened as his eyes landed on her. "What the fuck did you do?"

Oh shit!

She hated when he asked her questions. Ones she was never able to answer correctly. Whatever she said always made it worse. Not speaking was even worse than saying something wrong though, because then, according to Liam, she had something to hide.

Jenna cleared her throat. "What do you mean? I haven't done any—"

"Don't fucking lie to me." His voice was deep and gravelly. Filled with hate and… disgust.

A whimper was torn from her. She hated that he

had this effect on her.

He took a step towards her and she flinched back, her rear hitting the closed door. Liam sucked in a deep breath, his eyes moving away from her for just a second before returning. "I'm only going to ask you one more time... I hate it when you make me hit you. Why do you make me hit you, Jen-doll?" He used his pet name for her, which only made this whole thing so much worse.

If he hated hitting her, why the hell did he do it? Jenna licked her lips. "You don't have to hit me, Liam. Let's please talk about whatever it is that's made you so upset."

"I hope you're not trying to tell me what to do."

She shook her head. "I would never do that. Please—"

"Besides," he cut her off, "I'm not the one with something to say, Jenna. There is no need for a goddamn heart-to-heart. Start talking. Make it quick. I'm about to lose my fucking temper." His lean muscles coiled beneath his shirt and his fists grew ever tighter.

If only she knew what he wanted to hear. She would tell him in a heartbeat. Anything to avoid what was about to happen.

His eyes moved about the room before settling back on her. They had that crazy look about them that she had come to know so well. His eyes narrowed. "Why the fuck did Anthony say you had a tight ass? What does Anthony know about your ass?"

No way! Hell no!

She was about to get beaten because one of his

asshole friends had noticed her butt? Jenna did everything she could to avoid getting noticed by other guys. She wore her clothes a size too big. She always made sure her butt was covered. She'd even taken to wearing tight sports bras to conceal her big-ass boobs. There wasn't too much more she could do short of wearing a box and a mask. She'd cut her hair to her shoulders and didn't wear make-up. Not even lip gloss. The only time she dressed up was at home. He liked her in skimpy, revealing outfits when it was just for him. Never if she set foot outside of the house though. Yet, Liam was about to beat her because one of his friends had still, by some miracle, noticed that she had a tight ass. More like skinny ass since she didn't eat that well any more. Living with a psychopath would do that to a person.

"I have no idea why he would say that. Why don't you ask him?" The words just slipped out. His insinuation coupled with his placing all the blame on her irritated the crap out of her. The emotion was quickly replaced by more fear though as his face turned red.

"I'm asking you!" He punched her in the gut, causing her to double over. All the air left her lungs and her eyes began to water as pain radiated through her. The guy could pack a serious punch.

It took a few seconds before she could breathe again. After filling her lungs a few times, she lifted her gaze to meet his. Her body was still a bit hunched. *Oh boy!* Normally after he punched her, he calmed down a little. Not this time. "Tell me why he said it and don't fucking lie this time."

There was nothing she could say that would appease him. She pulled in a deep breath, trying to prepare herself for the onslaught. When she'd stalled long enough, she looked him square in the eye, even though it went against every instinct. "I have no idea why he would say such a thing. Maybe because he's a guy and guys—" Jenna didn't get to finish her sentence.

Liam snarled through clenched teeth. His eyes were wild, reminding her of a rabid animal. Not that she'd ever seen one, but she was sure this was how it would look. She took another hard punch to the stomach and was sure that her spleen had burst. The pain was excruciating.

There was no time to dwell because he punched her again, this time on the side of her ribs. Liam often hit her just below her breasts and under her arms. That way, it was easy to conceal the bruises. What the asshole didn't understand was that trying to function normally with busted up ribs was almost impossible. Another meaty punch, a bit higher this time. Thankfully she didn't hear a crack. Bruising she could handle, a break was a whole other ballgame, since Liam didn't allow her to go to the emergency room. Couldn't have people asking a whole lot of questions not after… the pain of the memory that blossomed inside of her was far worse than any beating her loser boyfriend could inflict and she hardly felt the next punch.

She only registered that he had hit her in the face when her mouth filled with blood and she hit the door behind her with a crack to the back of her scalp. He normally never touched her face or any other part that was difficult to conceal.

"Look what you made me do," Liam growled. He slapped her with an open hand that sent her sprawling on the cold tiles.

She watched him advance from the corner of her eye, realizing that he wasn't done with her. She pulled herself into a tight ball.

Liam kicked her on her lower back. It hurt so badly. It was only once he finished laying in on her that she realized she was sobbing. Saying the word *please* over and over again. "God dammit, Jen-doll." She could hear him pacing but didn't have the energy to look.

Her face was wet from her tears and her nose streamed.

"Look what you made me do. It's only because I love you so damned much." He leaned in next to her, stroking the hair from her face. "Oh god… look at you." He made a pained noise. "Shit! I'm so sorry. I know you didn't do anything with Anthony." He continued to stroke her hair. "I know you wouldn't do that to me…" his voice hardened and so did his hold on her hair. It stung, causing more tears to leak from her eyes.

It was only when she groaned that he finally let her go.

"Jen-doll… baby… I love you so much," he cooed.

He sure had a great way of showing it.

"Let's get you cleaned up." He rose to his feet and disappeared for a few minutes. When he returned, he had a warm, wet cloth which he used to mop up her blood. *How thoughtful of him.*

Next, he grabbed the first aid kit and used some sort of alcohol-based antiseptic to clean her busted lip. Lastly, he gave her two white pills. "For the pain," his voice was soft and caring. "Here..." He handed her a glass of water and helped her into a sitting position so that she could drink.

Jenna tried not to look at him. She tried not to cry out or moan. It hurt to breathe. It hurt to move. It just hurt... period. Her back was the worst. A dull ache had taken up residence deep inside her. She was a little concerned that he may have done serious damage.

"Fucking hell, Jen... I'm so sorry." He continued to whisper soft shit about how much he cared and how amazing she was. His one hand cupped her chin while his other hand trailed down her arm.

All she could do was pray that he left her alone. *Please, God.* "I'm really sore." She winced as her lip pulled.

"I said I was sorry." His muscles bunched and his eyes flashed with anger. This was such a ridiculous situation. Liam hated it if she showed pain or discomfort after her beatings. It obviously made him feel guilty, which was unacceptable. *What a dickhead!*

She tried to smile but it hurt her split lip too much. Jenna felt a warm trickle on her chin as the cut reopened from her efforts.

Thankfully he ignored the blood, his eyes firmly on hers.

"I know you are... baby," she forced the words out, trying to hold back the vomit. "It's just that I think that maybe I should rest a bit." He always liked to have sex after he beat her. Either he got off on hurting her, or it was his sick way of making it up to her. Probably a little bit of both. It was utter hell, like a form of torture. To have to lie there while he—Jenna swallowed thickly. Trying to stop the churning in her belly. Aside from hating that he touched her, she really didn't think her battered body could handle it.

His expression softened. "Let's get you into bed. You rest up. You'll be as good as new in a few days."

Yeah right. Jenna nodded. "Thank you." Bile tasted bitter on her tongue. "I need to sleep. I'm really tired."

It would probably take weeks for her to heal. He might just ruin everything for her.

Jenna had to clench her teeth to stop herself from crying out when he lifted her. She buried her face in his shirt so that he wouldn't hear her panting. Sweat beaded on her forehead. Shit, Liam had really hurt her this time.

Printed in Poland
by Amazon Fulfillment
Poland Sp. z o.o., Wrocław